RADICAL OR NOT, HERE I COME

*One man's search for spiritual affirmation
and to understand radical Islam*

By E. LEROY NEAL

CONTENTS

This book is dedicated to my heroes

HEROES
by E. L. Neal

Heroes are a most curious kind.
We want to know them, and so we ask,
Are they God-like specters, selected by time,
Or ordinary people, assigned divine task?

And so it is, in our humanly way
Everyone is held to the light for scrutiny.
We slice them and dice them in every way known,
To measure and test their purity.

St. Paul fought the good fight, Luther took his stand,
Roosevelt charged up that hill in a foreign land.
Looking for heroes, we comb the past,
Unaware that many are close at hand.

Just what do we respect most in each man,
Cunning or warmth or strength of hand?
Or do the scales slide this way and that,
First a hero, then fool when he takes a stand?

My personal heroes have been easy to choose,
Without need of validation,
They are everyday people,
Who have known my own situation.

Coach Bush was my mentor, more than any man.
He saw something in me no other had seen.
He trained, tuned and tinkered with my body and brain,
Creating success and much-needed self-worth.

When I think of Lynn Thompson, and I often do,
Common horse sense and tenacity come to mind.
Then nostalgia overwhelms me as I weep inside,
Remembering how he faced death with such dignity.

Dr. Fred Kasch was chairman of my Thesis.
He modeled Christian values for me.
He taught me the joy of serving others
Then pointed out my final place in eternity.

And finally, Grady Neal, my father, my dad,
Who took life's cards, dealt from the bottom of the deck
And never whined about what he didn't have,
He simply became the best man he could possibly be.

These are my heroes, such as they are.
These are the men who have meant the most to me.
Not an unusually gifted bunch but remember,
God can raise up sons of Abraham from just such stones.

ACKNOWLEDGEMENTS

*"For I have come to have much joy and comfort
in your love, because the hearts of the saints have
been refreshed through you brother." (Philemon 7)*

O f all my many regrets, the lack of appreciation I had for so many great friends, coaches, and fabulous teammates, ranks very high. I did not understand their value at the time. Some of them will recognize small evidences of their own idiosyncrasies and personality traits in my friend Herman. This was not an accident because every one of them was instrumental in the person I became. If I could capture time with bottle and cork, I would use it to return to Fullerton High School in 1959, where I would personally thank Leonard Dickey, Jim Salmon, Patty Thompson, Mike Marenco, and a few others for putting up with me and my rather large head. I remember them often with great fondness.

At Fullerton Junior College I would tell Chuck Baer, Jan Underwood, and Harry McCalla that they were the "salt of the earth" to me and I envied their strength of character, while together we set the track world on it's ear. They were more than friends; they were inspirations at the time of my greatest need to be inspired.

To my teammates at Occidental College, I can only say that I felt like an ant next to their colossal achievements. Steve Haas was never aware of how much I watched him and thought of him as "quietly great." My roomie, Dixon Farmer, was the ultimate competitive and successful athlete, coach, teacher, and a great friend in spite of my sometimes negative outlook on life. Ron 'Whit' Whitney and his Oakie'isms was "one of a kind" and I admired him hugely. All three were world-class athletes, but more important, world-class people.

Ruth and Lynn Thompson were surrogate parents and I would tell them how much that meant to me though I never spoke of it at the time. They showed me how an intact and loving family faces the challenges all families face sooner or later. In addition to all the other things they did for me, Lynn taught me how to fashion a Windsor knot for my tie and Ruth showed me what a great friend a mother can be.

Phil Thomas and Ray Steffanus, my co-workers at LA County are very special people to me. Phil showed me that intelligence, curiosity and logic were ever bit as important to solving problems as graduate degrees from prestigious universities. Ray was the personification of living life without apology. The fact that I never took him up on his offer to "go have a beer" in place of a wedding is no reflection of my love for his friendship.

I do not have to rely on time travel to thank Coach Jim Bush. We call each other quite often and I usually get to visit him whenever I am in California. Our relationship was very unique. Not because he was a world famous coach at the time (which he did become) or that I was an Olymipic runner but exactly the opposite. Our closeness was due to Father Time. Our conjoined careers profited from the timing of when we worked together. He was a young lion and quickly rising, type A, success oriented coach. I was his willing lump of clay that he used to refine his coaching system and principles. During our time together he matured and developed his talents in the intricacies of coaching and I learned discipline, dedication and the willingness to postpone gratification for a future worthwhile goal. I benefited most from his very steep learning curve

Dr. Fred Kasch was a pioneer in adult fitness and cardiac patient rehabilitation and baptized me into the exciting machinations of the Exercise Physiology Laboratory. He took my natural curiosity and thirst for learning then refined it and gave it direction. Under his influence I began to appreciate serving others above self-indulgence. His rock solid example of Christian Leadership inspired me to think outside of myself.

To Shannon, I owe so much because she knew me when I was at my worst in how I treated and used others. In spite of that she did not give up on me until I knew the saving grace of Jesus Christ.

Without a doubt, my father was the most influential person in my life. When I "look in the mirror, what do I see . . . grey hair and dancing eyes . . . I've become he." His witticisms, work ethic, visions of what is possible . . . just about everything I now do is a virtual carbon copy that oozes out of me at every turn.

I must also give praise and thanks to Dr. George Naeem Guirguis for his scholarly review of my discussions about Muslims, Islam and the Koran. His expertise and knowledge were invaluable in helping me to a better understanding of them.

Encouragement and advice from Pastor Doug Brauner was gratefully received. Very importantly, he helped me keep my theological excursions within the boundaries of solid Bible interpretation.

And finally, to Gail, my life partner who has supported me in everything, I have to shout from the rooftops that her love relationship with Jesus has never failed to pull me back from the precipice of doubt or discouragement. She continues to inspire me every day.

God bless and keep every one of you.

PROLOGUE

---※---

So He was saying, "What is the kingdom of God
like, and to what shall I compare it? It is like a
mustard seed, which a man took and threw into
his own garden; and it grew and became a tree,
and the birds of the air nested in it's branches."
(Luke 13:18–19)

S eminal events, poignant moments, great books and inspira-
tional people provide important building blocks of a person's
life. At the time, we often don't recognize them for the impact
they have. It is only later, looking back that we begin to appreciate how crucial they were to the final product, us, who we are
and what we have become. Living life in the moment is too fast,
too confusing, just too much of everything to be fully understood at the time. And, as I soon found out, this building block

process never stops, not even when we reach the penultimate age of seventy-three.

In January of 2015 two of my "blocks" landed on me with a thud, creating a thirst to learn in a very specific area and near panic to re-evaluate my faith and worldview. The first was a sermon in which the pastor quoted Acts 9:4–5, the conversion of Saul on the road to Damascus. I had never considered how "radical" that conversion was. This epiphany jarred my memory, reminding me of multiple headlines describing "radical" Muslims. The term, radical, was burned into my brain and drove to me read, *Seeking Allah, Finding Jesus* and *Son of Hamas,* my second block. In both books the authors describe Muslim "radicals" and compare Islam to Christianity.

Suddenly I was confronted with two problems. First, Saul's complete and dramatic reversal was arguably the most radical conversion in the history of Christianity while my personal conversion was notably quiet. I felt very small next to Saul. This comparison challenged my understanding of Christian conversion. My faith had never been challenged before and I needed to reevaluate my personal conversion and very importantly, the depth of my commitment. Second, I was embarrassed at how unprepared I was to defend my own faith in comparison to Islam.

The primary tension I needed to resolve was to determine if Muslims were too radical or was I not radical enough.

I decided to write a book in order to explore possible answers to the questions that now tattooed my brain. It seemed the best way to engage my catharsis and in the process learn about Islam. In recognition that it had taken a lifetime to come up with these questions and to make my book more believable, I chose to use my personal journey to faith as the vehicle for this "building block" review. This account is factual. However, I had never kept a diary or even practiced journaling. I had crystal clear recollections of some events but only fuzzy awareness of the multitude of others and the many people I had interacted with. So, conversations with my friend Herman Reyhadi, are fictitious composites of all my relationships, life experiences and research. The other people you meet, the antidotes and historical notes are all true, although an alias will be used here and there to protect those who might not want to participate in my narrative. I will tell my story by paraphrasing conversations I've had, books I have read and events in my life in the fifty-six years since I graduated from high school in 1959.

The reader is cautioned on textual mechanics and content. The narrative will not roll easily along in chronological order. When necessary, I will take the liberty to "time travel" with no regard for the calendar. Content trumped a strict timeline. And sometimes, cited references will be out of sync. with the time period of the discussion at hand. Please note, the date and time announced at the beginning of each chapter are placed there to alert the reader to these time shifts. Also, although connected by several common threads, each chapter could be read independently or even out of order. All Biblical references are from the New American Standard Bible translation except in Appendix B (King James version). Finally, this is not a textbook on comparative religions or apologetics; it is my story with supporting facts.

My curiosity and belief that God invited me to this task led me to ask:

1. Is there a significant difference between Islam and Christianity? If so, how are they different?

2. Is there evidence that the Koran and the Bible are essentially the same or strikingly different in unity, prophecy, inerrancy and understandability? Can either stand alone, without supplemental references or commentaries?

3. What are the dynamics of "radical" conversion in both religions? What is the unmet need that drives one to conversion in either case?

4. Is Islam truly a "religion of peace"? Is Christianity more militant and violent than commonly professed or admitted?

5. Was my non-dramatic conversion as powerful as more radical/dramatic Christian conversions?

6. Why was I so unprepared to rationally discuss these comparisons with my counterpart, a sincere Muslim?

Chapter 1

MY JOURNEYS BEGIN

California Bound

*The priest said to them, "Go in peace; your way
in which you are going has the Lord's approval."
(Judges 18:6)*

**Wednesday, January 7, 2015, 9:00 AM, Denver
International Airport:** The Frontier Airlines terminal at
DIA is very crowded. Outside it has turned into a full blizzard.
Visibility is down to about ten feet and announcements of delays
have begun. Flight 405 to LAX via Denver has not left Salt Lake
City and is not expected until further notice. It is now snowing
so hard it would take a miracle just to get back to my truck at
the long term parking lot, a mere five miles away. I am stuck

and there is no way to know for how long. This is Colorado in January.

I have mixed feelings about my trip. Physically, I am headed to my mother's house in Fullerton, California (see Appendix A, 1). But in reality it is only the occasion for two other journeys I have just now begun. One is intellectual as I begin my research into radical Islam. The other is spiritual as I retrace the steps that led me to a total Christian transformation. My trip to California is out of family duty. My intellectual and spiritual journeys, seeking information and affirmation are personal; they are necessary for my peace of mind.

In addition to normal travel anxieties there are other challenges that have increased my angst more than usual. As a primary caregiver and legal representative of my ninety-six-year-old mother I am looking forward to visiting with her and my sister Sherrill who does the lion's share of the day-to-day work taking care of Mom but dreading the legal wrangling with lawyers and facing a judge to represent her interests in the Neal Family Trust due to her being declared incompetent in 2004.

These visits conjure up waves of nostalgia as well as a sense of futility. Many great memories of my growing years are relived each visit but Mom has severe dementia and she doesn't know whom she is talking to from one minute to the next. Physically, she has great vital signs of blood pressure, heart rate, and blood chemistries and her diabetes is well under control. But she is an invalid and it is very difficult to take care of her. If I don't go, my sister will have to face all the work taking care of Mom and the legal struggles as well, alone. I have to go.

Timing of the trip could not be worse. Flights out of Denver in January are tenuous at best and my heart and mind are in a different place altogether. This trip will interrupt the excitement of my research and writing I have just now begun for a book. I have to console myself that at least I can do a lot of targeted reading as well as consulting with seasoned book writers I know in California. This helps to calm me as I begin my frenetic search for answers to the questions triggered by last Sunday's sermon. Those questions are the heart and soul of my book.

My faith journey was kick-started in 1959 by my friend, Herman Reyhadi, who laid the groundwork for my eventual conversion to an unapologetic Christian faith. In fits and stops, I stumbled around for thirty-two years, avoiding direct contact with God until I finally gave in from exhaustion. Like many others, as a kid I had been a "nominal" or "cultural" Christian. I suspect there are a large number "cultural Muslims" as well. My Dad had a Southern Baptist bent and Mom had been raised in the Church of Christ but I didn't take any of it to heart. I went to church because my family went. It was what families did in the late '40s and early '50s. We attended church somewhat regularly until the six of us kids entered Junior and Senior High School. From then on we went our separate ways. I continued to go to church but it was mostly for social reasons. I tended to gravitate to the Protestant church where the largest number of cute girls attended or in one case, a specific, very cute girl.

However, in 1955 I met Herman Reyhadi at Fullerton Union High School. He was a second generation Pakistani and a committed, on fire, Christian Believer. By the time we graduated in 1959, he had begun to chip away at my resistance to becoming more than a nominal Christian. Looking back, my eventual coming to faith as well as an awareness of Islam really began at Buddy's Burgers, just after graduation. It was there where Herman's family story and his continuous teaching, preaching and personal encouragement finally began to penetrate my stubborn and arrogant shell. As you will see, it took fourteen years to complete the process.

As we shared lunch that day, he planted some very important seeds that I would refer back to in many future situations. He had awakened my curiosity about God's Word. Years later I was surprised at how familiar I was with scripture and how comfortable it made me feel. Herman had laid the most important cornerstone of my life.

But I can't escape the irony of this trip. It is a very normal trip thousands of others take on a regular basis. Yet for me it is a return to the place where my faith journey and a neophyte's understanding of Islam began as well as a family visit. Literally everything started at that hamburger stand in 1959.

That's What Friends Are For

"Bear one another's burdens, and thus fulfill the law of Christ." (Galations 6:2)

Buddy's Burgers was a lunchtime institution for Fullerton High School students. It was conveniently located one block due West of the school. Most students usually ate on campus but sooner or later almost everyone went to Buddy's for lunch, out of boredom with the cafeteria or just to get off campus for a while. It was not a little thing that Buddy's also had the best burgers in town. It was a walk-up venue. There was no indoor dinning, just two picnic tables next to the small North facing building on the South West corner of Chapman and what was then called Spadra Road (today it is Harbor Blvd.).

I remember that Monday, two months removed from all the hoopla of graduation. My best friend for the last four years, Herman Reyhadi and I were waiting for our usual Cheeseburger w/onions, fries and a coke. I was somewhat uneasy about our meeting. I knew that we both had to move on despite the disruption in our friendship but I wondered if we would remain such good friends. However, for the moment I was hungry and enjoyed the aroma of the feast to come.

We were subdued and pensive while we waited for our orders. A lot of things in our lives were about to change dramatically and the reality of those changes had us both feeling a little insecure. It was probably the last time we would meet for who knew how long. Adding to my disquiet, I felt pretty small and self-conscious compared to Herman. He was the poster boy for successful students and I was the epitome of "just another jock."

When we got our orders we ate in silence. Finally, as we finished Herman began to shift his weight around and shuffle the paper plates and cups. Looking at nothing in particular he began with a throw away comment, "Well I guess this is it! I wish we could be closer, but there are vacations."

He was stalling. I thought oh, oh, here comes one of his famous sermons. So I beat him to the punch. "Herman, there are a couple of things I have wanted to ask you for a long time. We have talked a lot about our families but I have never heard a complete explanation of how your Mom and Dad became Christians. I don't know that much about different religions but it seems to me there isn't a big difference between Christianity and Islam. They accept many of the same Old Testament scriptures and Patriarchs, they claim the New Testament (Injeel in Arabic) was sent to Jesus by God (Allah), they profess a peaceful religion, they believe in an after life, I mean they pretty much sound just like us don't they? So I was wondering why your parents converted. Aren't they all (religions) about the same? What did they gain by such a dramatic cultural change?"

My tactic was shrewd. It was based on my knowledge of what we shared and where we went in opposite directions. We had become friends while sitting together in French I our freshman year but we couldn't have been more different. It was that difference that was the core of why we were such good friends. Like ham and eggs go together but are distinctly different, we were a strong team and complemented each other. I was appealing to his habit of wanting to "educate" me whenever he could plus I really was interested in his parent's story. They had emigrated to the U.S. from Pakistan after converting to Christianity. His father was an engineer and his mother worked in chemical research for a large pharmaceutical company. They settled in Fullerton and

Herman was born in the Cottage Hospital located just two blocks North of where we now sat. His parents named him Herman in honor of a British friend who had led them to Christ. He was an only child.

My parents came from Arkansas and Oklahoma. Dad was a carpenter then later a contractor. Mom kept the company financial records and drew the blueprints for Dad's jobs. There were six of us Neal kids and everyone within a half-mile of our house knew exactly when we were home.

I had enjoyed some success as a track athlete (third in the Mile in the 1958 California State Championship) but carried a miserable GPA of only 1.8, just barely good enough to stay eligible for athletics. My GPA would have been lower had it not been for the A's I got in Physical Education, Wood Shop, Photography, Drivers Education, Mechanical Drawing and other 'basket weaving' classes. I had been recruited by USC, UCLA, Long Beach State University, the Naval Academy, and a few of the smaller colleges. But my senior year was a total disappointment on the track. Repeated bouts of the flu proved too much and I didn't qualify for the CIF (California Interscholastic Federation) regional meet, let alone the State Championship. I was not the star runner of the previous year and the recruiters quit calling as soon as they saw my GPA. My SAT score was worse than my grades and post high school options had dried up quickly.

Herman was captain of the Debate Team, Head Yell Leader, President of the French Club, the Art Club and Hi Yi (Christian club). Academically he was a giant. He had nearly maxed the SAT and carried a 3.95, four-year GPA (he got a few Bs in Physical Education) while taking Calculus, Chemistry and Physics and traveling to France as an American Field Service, Exchange Student. When he returned home from Europe his favorite phrase was "Mon petite chou!" (loosely translated, "My little cabbage." It was a very sweet line to use on a girl) and he drank "café au lait" by the gallons.

He was also president of the youth group at our church and spent a few weeks every summer at Hume Lake, a Christian Camp in Central California. When he came home from camp he was always bubbling over with new scriptures he had memorized and couldn't wait to share them with me. I often called him Herman Neutics because after camp he invariably had a few special sermons, just for his best friend.

And now, he was packed and ready to leave in two days to drive back East where he would attend Princeton on an academic scholarship in Political Science. I was registered at FJC (Fullerton Junior College) straight across the street from the high school where there was no need for scholarships. Tuition was $35.00 per semester plus $13.50 for your Student Body Card and you bought your own books. But the final humiliation was the fact I would have to enroll in and successfully complete "Dumbbell English" before I could even declare a major and begin any of the disciplines available.

My ploy appeared to be working, as he seemed to become totally absorbed in answering my questions. But his next sentence caught me off guard.

"I'm really glad you asked that because there is something I have wanted to talk to you about, myself."

I was trapped. I should have known better. With all his experience as a champion debater, he had not come close to losing sight of his original goal. "Oh really? What is it?" I answered weakly.

He went on. "I'm going to answer your questions but first this gives me the opportunity to bring up something I have dreaded doing for a long time."

This was headed in a bad direction. I braced myself for the coming lecture.

"Leroy, you know I have considered you my best friend for years. And attending church together has only cemented our friendship but, as a true friend, I have to point out some things I know about you because I care enough to help you any way I can."

I sat there stunned with mixed feelings. I had always looked up to Herman as the Rock of Gibraltar. In every situation it had always been him and me against all comers. Now I was about to get a dressing down similar to the ones I got from my father. What followed was a devastating and sobering personal evaluation.

"First let me ask you an off the wall question. Suppose you were to die today and stand before God and He were to ask you, 'Why should I let you into my heaven?' (Kennedy question #44 from the *Evangelism Explosion*) What would you say?"

For a few moments I was speechless as I desperately searched my cognitive brain cells for the "right" answer. Finding no help there I struck out on my own. "Well, I guess I would say that I attend church fairly regular, I've been a pretty decent person and haven't murdered..."

"Burrrrrrrrrrt!" came his best impression of the buzzer going off on a quiz show or basketball game! **"Wrong!"**

I was puzzled.

He continued. "I was afraid that would be your answer. But being a good person who acts with morals and restraint is not enough. And there is no way you can ever be good enough or earn your way into heaven. It just doesn't work that way." He pulled out a Lindy pen from his pocket protector, grabbed a napkin and quickly scribbled down some Bible verses (John 3:16–18, John

14:6–7, Acts 4:12, 2 Timothy 3:14–15, Ephesians 2:8–10 and Titus 3:4–7) and handed them to me. He finished the thought. "As your friend I think you need to study these scriptures until you come up with the right answer for yourself." From there it got worse.

"I have watched you for four years in all situations. But I have never heard you pray out loud. I have never known of you attending a Bible study. You have never gone on a long-term or even a short-term mission. You have never brought a friend to church and even though you were baptized right here in our own church I have never heard you profess Jesus Christ as your Lord and Savior. I have dreaded bringing these things up but I am really hurting that you don't have the same confidence and joy I have. Oh, you seem to be happy enough, but I think it is all window dressing. I can read people pretty well and I don't think you are truly happy. I think that you have an empty space in your life that you try to fill up with athletics and girlfriends," he averred. At this I was shamed into silence. All I could do was hang my head and stare at my shoes.

He then changed course. "Leroy, you are going over to FJC and I am headed to Princeton. Now I am not your Daddy, but I won't be around to help you, either. So I want to give you some advice. The rest is up to you and God. Now this might sound like it's coming from left field but do you remember that day about a year ago, when we took your Dad's truck and just started driving through the orange orchards North of town? I promise to connect the dots in a few minutes. Remember how we were driving along that creek just North of the old Sunny Hills Barn?" How could I forget that day? It was the closest thing to a catastrophe I had ever experienced. We were lucky to escape with our arms and legs intact.

The truck Herman referred to was my Dad's second pickup. He had bought a new Ford F-150 and I inherited the 1951, faded blue Studebaker, half-ton pickup with a three quarter-ton box, a lumber rack and double overload springs. It was closer to a buckboard than a motor vehicle. It was not particularly sporty but it got twenty miles per gallon and I was free to use it 24/7.

Everything was going just fine that day until we drove along the creek approaching the tunnel that ran under Spadra Road. About 100 yards ahead, at the far side of the tunnel we saw a fence with a closed gate. It was a very narrow truck path and there was no place to turn around with the creek on our right and a steep hill to the left. I decided to back up rather than going all the way to the gate, which in all probability was locked and would then have to back up even further. This was a big mistake. As I began to back up I lost view of the creek. You can probably guess what happened next. I got too close to the creek bank and suddenly it gave way. The right rear tire sank and stopped just short of the creek. The left front tire was about a foot in the air and the rear axel was solidly grounded. We were stuck. I tried to drive out but the back wheels just spun around throwing rocks into the creek.

When we got out to inspect we quickly realized how close to an absolute disaster we had come. The only thing that saved us from a complete rollover was a load of pea gravel in the truck bed left over from one of Dad's jobs. Without that ballast we would probably have come to rest upside down in the middle of the creek. And we didn't have seat belts in those days. We concluded the only solution was to dig our way out. But after searching behind the seat, where shovels were usually stored, looking in the bed and then looking at each other, we began to really worry. No shovels, no mattocks, no tools at all; not even a claw hammer or a screwdriver. You have to remember, we didn't have cell phones in 1958. We were two miles from town and about three or four miles from the nearest gas station. We had a big problem.

Herman saved the day. "Leroy, don't you carry some ping pong paddles with you for Wednesday night games at the church?" I looked under the shotgun seat and there they were. We began digging with the paddles and started laughing at our situation.

Within a minute or two we were howling. We became absolutely proud of ourselves for our ingenuity and resourcefulness. It took about an hour to dig enough of the bank out to clear the axel. Then we threw some pea gravel in front of both back tires. IT WORKED! One try and we were back on the truck path with the shinny side up. The final irony however, was we decided to go up to the gate rather than repeat our first mistake. It was a late Sunday afternoon with no one around and we figured we could just break out if we had to. Imagine our surprise when we got to the gate and there was no chain and no lock.

"Well if that don't beat a hen a peckin' with a wooden bill, I don't know what does!" As much as my Dad's Ozark humor usually embarrassed me, it would slip out, automatically and unannounced at just about any time. We opened the gate and drove home.

Now, back at Buddy's we grinned at each other as we remembered the incident. But what was Herman's point? "Leroy, remember how helpless we felt when we didn't have the right tools? The right tools would have made a big difference. We were lucky to get out of that predicament."

"OK," I replied, "so, connect the dots for me."

"Sure. You just asked me some questions about Islam and Christianity. If you had the right tools you would have already known the answers. You are going to run into a lot of new situations in the next few years and if you don't have the right tools, life is going to leave you stuck like that old truck. You will only survive out of pure luck."

Now I was really puzzled. "So what tools are you talking about? Where do I get them?"

His answer was simple and direct. "The Bible! You have to memorize scripture. The Bible has an explanation for everything. It is the best tool anyone can ever have." This sounded like an enormous task. Memorize the Bible?

Herman tried to calm my fears. "Memory work is only difficult because we are lazy and don't do it enough. Ancient cultures memorized their entire histories. Some of the Old Testament came from an oral tradition and it is accurate. If you commit scripture to memory a whole new world is going to open up for you. You will have the right tools no matter what you face. Isaiah 55:11–12 gives us the promise that God's Word will accomplish His purpose. His words will not return to Him empty. And His purpose for you is, that 'You will go out with joy and be led with peace.' Herman went on, "It works just like a compass to point you in the right direction. Learn to depend on it."

Looking back now I can see how Herman's antidote influenced me many years later. He had shown me how to use God's

Word as an everyday prescription for life. Often, in the period before I confessed Jesus Christ as Lord, I would find myself evaluating things I said and did through the light of scripture. The cornerstone was now permanently fixed in place. I was not yet ready to turn my life completely around but I certainly was beginning to believe in God, Christ and the Holy Spirit. The evidence was everywhere but I didn't have the faith of even a mustard seed that I would qualify for such generous terms. I knew the darkness of my soul.

Will The Real Islam Please Stand Up?

"Beloved, do not believe every spirit, but test the spirits to see whether they are from God; because many false prophets have gone out into the world."
(I John 4:1)

"Now I will tell you how my parents became Christians. The first thing you have to understand is that Islam is the State, politically and theologically. Here in the US we have separation of Church and State. In Pakistan and other Muslim countries, their Ayatollahs, Military Dictators or Muslim Monarchs control everything and they can be tyrannical. Islam is incompatible with democracy and they will tell you that, themselves. Zaid Shakir, the former Muslim Chaplin at Yale has said, 'Every Muslim who is honest would say, I would like to see America become a Muslim country … because Muslims can't accept the American Constitution since … it goes against the orders and ordainments of Allah.'[1] Sheikh Hamza Yusuf, his Co-founder of Zaytuna, a Muslim College in California, has 'railed against the "false gods" of democracy and the Bill of Rights, accuses Judaism of being racist and claims that Hugo Chaves, Manuel Noriega, Muammar Qaddafi, Saddam Hussein and Osama Bin Laden and the Taliban are all victims of United States aggression.'[2] If you value separation of church and state, you cannot support or even tolerate Fundamental Islam!

"In fact strict Sharia law results in the state running everyone's life to the point of fanaticism. They tell you what you can and can't do until the cows come home because Islam depends on external forces to control behavior whereas Christianity relies on self-control and personal accountability. Muslims are so afraid of some one else sinning you would think, 'they protest too much!' It actually reminds me a little bit of the strict moral codes of Puritanism in 17th century New England. This was the initial problem for my parents. They were very moral and upright Muslims and still they felt the heavy hand and restrictiveness of Sharia law." This had a ring of authenticity to it but Muslim countries were a long way off. They seemed remote to the point of irrelevancy.

"My parents are very well educated, professional people. Dad got his Engineering degree in England and worked for the British building irrigation systems and dams. Mom studied Chemistry in Australia and ran her own pharmaceutical store. They had always been diligent Muslims in prayer, giving to the poor and attending their Mosque. They were absolutely the proto-type of what we would today call 'moderate' Muslims. They had always depended on the three sources of Islamic instructions on life, the Koran, the Sira (biographies of the life of Muhammad) and the Hadith (traditional written reports of the actions and sayings of Muhammad), often referred to as the Islamic Trilogy. When they studied overseas they heard from alternative sources that disagreed with what they had always embraced about Islam.

"They began to wonder about Islam and what they had always believed without question as a matter of fact. They started to read the Koran, the Sira and the Hadith more critically. It was quite a shock to them when they came to a Hadith verse where Muhammad clearly stated that he had been ordered by Allah to fight against people until they convert to Islam in order that they 'will save (their) property and life from me.'[3] The blunt

39

aggressiveness of that position is also found in Surah (Koran) 9:29–30 where Allah said, 'Make war upon such of those whom the scriptures have been given (Israelites and Christians) as believe not in God or in the Last Day, and who forbid not that which God and His Apostle (Muhammad) have forbidden, and who profess not the profession of the truth, until they pay tribute out of hand and are humbled ... God do battle with them! How they are misguided!' If that doesn't make it clear enough we can look at another Hadith verse where, 'The messenger of Allah said, 'Kill those who change their religion.'[4] Sahih al-Bukari is considered as one of the most reliable and trusted of all Hadith. In it, one of his companions verifies Muhammad's proclamation once again that 'Whoever changed his Islamic religion, then kill him.'[5] There are many other Hadith that state the punishment for Islamic apostasy is death and the Sira back them up. Story after story told them about a vengeful and intolerant Muhammad.

"They finally went 'over the edge' when they read about the Battle of the Trench where Muhammad beheaded 300 to 600 men and boys (some estimates are as high as 900) and then sold the women and small children into slavery.[6] The Muslims justified this on the basis that they had been attacked first. But this gets us into which came first, the chicken or the egg. The complete background involves Muhammad expelling two of the Jewish tribes in the area because he wanted to take over their dominance in the local trades and commerce and their attack upon Medina was in response to this unjust displacement.[7] More importantly, this was not the Prophet they had idolized all of their lives. But the gruesome details were right there in the most trusted and sacred accounts of the Muslim faith. And when Islam was compared to Christianity, point by point, theologically and practically they were overwhelmed with disappointment about the under performance of Islam. It was a clear case of 'you will know them by their fruits.' Islam required outward performances while Christianity relied on changes in the heart.[8]

"Their biggest disconnect, however, came when they reexamined the Islamic practice of abrogation. Abrogation is Islam's method of resolving apparent contradictions between verses in the sacred texts. This process dictates that resolution is achieved by giving more weight to the most recent revelation from Allah that is, 'later pronouncements of the Prophet declare null and void his earlier pronouncements.'[9] It is right there in the Koran itself in Surah 2.100 and Surah 16.104, where the replacing of one verse by another is justified as being better than the original. 'According to His (God's) own testimony God abrogated or cancelled certain verses in the Koran and replaced them with others, while somewhat unaccountably leaving the cancelled verses in the text.'[10] You might liken it to a smorgasbord. You go along the steam table and pick up what you want and leave the rest. Perhaps the next time, you pick something different and leave what you liked the first time through. Depending on your needs and preferences at a particular time (or discussion) you will choose parts of the Koran that support your position at that time. There is something for everyone in it at any given time. I am ashamed to say there are some that call themselves 'Christians' who do the same thing with the Bible.

"But the Koran, by itself does not tell the entire story. Although there are a number of violent verses, as a whole the Koran sounds like a somewhat peaceful religion. Comparatively it is much more peaceful sounding than the Bible, especially when compared to the Old Testament. However, alone it is not understandable. It is the combination of the Koran, the Hadith and the Sira that paint a picture of intolerance and war. When my parents compared certain verses in the Trilogy that proclaimed Islam as a peaceful religion with more recent verses, violence was the clear winner. This was not consistent with their peaceful outlook nor with the Muslim lives they had been living," Herman stated.

Here I simply had to interject with questions about one of the biggest stumbling blocks to parading Christianity as "holier than thou." The Crusades! I was not a great student of history, yet even I was acutely aware of how sensitive Muslims are about the Crusades, not to mention the Inquisition. Any discussion with a Muslim comparing Islam to Christianity will immediately dredge up memories of the Crusades and light a fuse to their indignation. "Herman, that all sounds really good about your parents. I mean, like you said, it is important for you to know you own Holy books. But how does a Christian answer a Muslim when he challenges you on the lack of credibility due to the Crusades? How do we reconcile some of the bad press Christianity got from the Crusades? Also, where do we go in the Bible to justify the use of the 'sword' when the Israelites entered the Promised Land? They were instructed to kill all of the inhabitants. Weren't they specifically instructed to 'utterly destroy them … and show no favor?' (Deuteronomy7:1–2). Doesn't it sound a little bit like the pot calling the kettle black?"

The look on Herman's face scared me just a little. "I am really shocked. You have been paying more attention than I gave you credit for. Those are great questions. They are spot on to this whole comparison and those very questions were not lost on my parents, either." He paused then began to unravel his answers to my questions. "Tell me, Mr. History Professor, when were the Crusades?"

I tried but couldn't recall the precise dates. I answered the best I could. "I'm not sure but it was something like a one hundred and fifty to two hundred year span from the first to the last Crusade. I think they were around the end of the Dark Ages."

Again, Herman was quite pleased, "Terrific! Actually the first was in 1096 AD and the last was 1291 AD.[11] Have you heard of any Crusades or anything like them lately? No? Correct ... sort of ... Muslims will claim that they are still going on as we speak. They will say that the creation of the State of Israel in 1948 was simply a continuation of the Crusades. They will point to the British occupation of Pakistan, Egypt and Saudi Arabia as a form of Crusades. To them, Islam is under attack and therefore they are justified to fight back. But they are ignoring the religious component of the Crusades while later occupations by the British and the formation of Israel were economic and political actions, not 'forced by the sword' conversion efforts."

This information had me confused. Did Muslims justify violence on the basis of modern Crusades?

Herman then asked, "What was the purpose of the Crusades?"

Again I searched my memory banks for the correct answer. "To reclaim the Holy Land, wasn't it?"

Herman's encyclopedic mind took over. "Actually, if you recall, Muslims had gradually taken over the Middle East, North

Africa, India and even Spain. They had effectively closed off the Mediterranean to Western Europe and divided Eastern and Western Christendom. One train of thought is the Crusades can be described as a defensive effort by the Pope to reunite Christendom and to reclaim Spain as well as to regain access to Jerusalem. They were not per se an attempt to convert anyone to Christianity. However, the Crusades were very poorly organized with little central control or discipline. Many of the Crusaders were motivated by a sense of adventure, conquest, power and fame. As a result, there were many atrocities in the name of God. Others were truly inspired by spiritual devotion but their efforts were misguided in the belief that God would help them win even though their mission had nothing to do with Biblical principles or directions from Jesus. In fact, the fourth Crusade only got as far as Constantinople. The Crusaders ran out of money and stopped to set up their own kingdom and began killing Eastern Christians.[12] The Crusades and the Inquisition were big mistakes for similar reasons.

"On the other hand, when was the last time you read or heard about Muslims using the 'sword' to convert anyone to Islam or to kill someone for trying to leave it?"

I shrugged my shoulders, "I really haven't paid much attention to that stuff. I don't remember any incidents like that."

Herman became very serious, "Well, I can tell you it happens a lot. My parents had to leave Pakistan for that exact reason. A more current example was when Vian Bakir Fatah was stabbed to death by her Iraqi ex-husband in Norway. Her crime … she had converted to Christianity and had a new boyfriend. Closer to home, a woman named Marlyn Hassan, who was eight months pregnant with twins, was stabbed to death in New Jersey by her husband for refusing to convert from Hinduism to Islam.[13] In Irving, Texas, sisters Sarah and Amina Said were seventeen and eighteen years old when their father shot and killed both of them because they were adopting Western ways of dressing rather than being veiled as called for by Islamic tradition. Their mother assisted in the murders.[14] Sixteen-year old Palestina, 'Tina' Isa was murdered by her father in St. Louis and in New York Waheed Allah Mohammad stabbed his nineteen-year-old sister, Fauzia, both cases for the same reason.[15] And in Atlanta, Kandeela Sandal was murdered by her father, because she wanted a divorce from her Muslim husband."[16]

Herman was almost in tears as he noted, "The number of honor killings is appalling. According to the United Nations there are about 5,000 of them per year, of just women, in Pakistan alone and worldwide numbers are much greater in this bloody category."[17] This was a stunning revelation to me. Suddenly, radical Islam and violence did not seem all that far away.

Herman continued to explain. "Now to answer your questions about a double standard where the sword is concerned, you need to know the context of those commands. God used the Israelites to 'utterly destroy' the inhabitants of the land because of their wicked practice of infanticide. They sacrificed children, even babies on their altars. Further, it was necessary to clean out the area to prevent the Israelites from adopting the same practices by association. It can also be argued those actions were defensive in that they were surrounded by hostile nations whose primary goal was to wipe them out. It has always been this way and continues to this day. The Arabs hate for the Jews has been center stage in the world for thousands of years dating back to when Hagar and Ismael fled into the desert to escape Sarah's wrath. (Genesis 16:5–6) But it was Muhammad's conflict with the local Jewish tribes of Mecca that accelerated that hatred to the current levels of rage and fanaticism against the Jews.

"It should be noted, the Israelites didn't use the sword to convert anyone to Judaism. And you will only see such disciplinary actions in the Old Testament. In the New Testament, Jesus gave us new marching orders, to love our enemies as ourselves. The Israelites were no longer Gods instrument to punish evil people.

You see, when Jesus came He bore the burden of Judgment and the warfare of God's people in the Old Testament became spiritual warfare in the New Testament."

At this I was somewhat confused. "Wait just one cotton pickin' minute. Isn't that abrogation, just like what you described about Islam?"

Herman smiled. "Good job, Leroy! I'm glad to see you are staying awake. There certainly are some similarities, aren't there. But there are subtle variances that make the two situations very different. In Islam, abrogation means you can throw out the original verses and replace them with Muhammad's most recent revelations. You can now, simply ignore the older ones. In the Bible, nothing is ever thrown out. Those verses are still relevant to the whole story. They explain how the Israelites lived out God's plan up to that point. And the later instructions from Jesus don't deny the history of what led up to His coming. His instructions are intended to teach us our role in God's plan, not change it or ignore it."

I was not quite convinced yet. "I can see there is a difference but I can also easily see it is subtle enough that a Muslim might not accept it as a 'good enough' answer."

Herman refined his explanation, "Yes, that could be a problem if that was all there was to it but think of it this way. The verses in the Koran are all specific directives from Allah to Muslims and by extension to you the reader. The verses in the Bible we are talking about were instructions to the Israelites, only. They were not intended as life instructions for the reader and therefore can be seen as an explanation of how God's plan was playing out. Nowhere is the reader told that he must kill his enemies or even any unbelievers, in order to please God but in Islam, that is exactly what the true Muslim is being told to do. The main lesson here is that the Israelites, and you, are always better off if you obey God. By comparison, every thing in the Koran is intended to be direct orders to Muslims from Allah. You see, 'violence is incidental to Judaism and Christianity and fundamental to Islam.'[18] Does that clear it up?"

I nodded my head. "Yes, I can see that. That does help but didn't you make a point a few minutes ago that apostasy in Islam is punishable by death." I kept up my adversarial push.

"Well now, you are getting testy. What are you referring to? Of course I've talked about that, many times."

I continued to push. "In Deuteronomy 13 the Israelites were instructed to kill family and friends if they 'fell away' as an act of honor, weren't they? So how do we distinguish between the 'good honor killings' in the Bible and those 'despicable honor killings' in the Koran?" For a moment I thought I had him on the ropes from his puzzled look.

"Well, if that don't beat a hen a peckin' with a wooden bill!" He murmured in mock surprise, teasing me with my own Ozark declarative. "When did you study Deuteronomy?"

"Just answer my question," I bantered back.

He wasn't ruffled in the least and calmly responded, "Well, it is much the same as we have just discussed about those other directives to the Israelites, in the context of that period of time. It's another example of how God instructed them to behave at that specific time for their own protection. But Jesus never directed us to kill anyone, not even for unbelief. He came to save the lost not to punish anyone. Now can I move on?"

Herman picked up his parents' story where I had interrupted. "Another area that became a problem for my parents was the dramatic difference between what they had believed about Muhammad's private life and what they were now finding out for themselves. When they began to dig deeper they discovered that when it was convenient, Muhammad would suddenly have a new revelation from Allah that benefitted Muhammad. One of the most famous events of this nature occurred when Muhammad, who had four wives already, decided he really liked Zaynab, the wife of his adopted son Zayd. But Islam allowed only four wives per man at the time. Suddenly, Muhammad had a new revelation and Allah granted him an exception.[19] Five wives were now OK for Muhammad but not for anyone else.[20] With this revelation, the adopted son saw the handwriting on the wall, divorced his wife and gave her to Muhammad. My parents did not like the duplicity," said Herman.

There was more. "In addition, there appeared to be two vastly different Muhammads. In the first 10–15 years of Islam, while he lived in Mecca, Muhammad seemed to be a very peaceful prophet. His revelations in this period were very conciliatory and forgiving, probably from a position of weakness. However, when he moved to Medina, he began to gain political and military strength and his revelations, more and more called for the blood and plunder of anyone who was not Muslim.

"They continued to study and made a great effort to resolve the growing number of inconsistencies they were discovering but it was impossible. They finally recognized that their idea of Islam and fundamental Islam were irreconcilable. What they did not understand was that in fact they were not truly Muslim. They thought they were. They tried very hard to be model Muslims. But the reality was, they were practicing a religion that did not exist!

"The fact that they were not main stream Muslims was driven home when members of their own family and local 'fundamentalists' (those who are 'faithful' to the tenets of their religion) began to criticize them in several areas. First, they were not happy with the equality in the marriage plus they didn't like the fact that a woman ran her own business. This is quite ironic because Islam relies very heavily upon Muhammad's personal example and his first wife, Kadija was very wealthy from her own merchant trade business. They also felt Dad's relationship with the British was suspicious at best and traitorous at worst. The fundamentalists especially did not like Mom's independence and habit of leaving home unattended by a male relative. When some Mutawain (roaming enforcers of Sharia Law) caught Mom alone on her way to the store they beat her with their staffs. When they beat her a second and third time, my parents were ready to listen to a British friend of Dad's who happened to be a Christian. He eventually convinced them to convert to Christianity."

Herman then proceeded to explain three monumental and exclusionary points that clearly separated Islam and Christianity. "The first principle of irreconcilable differences is the brutal, seventh century practice of punishment for apostasy. Fundamentalists in Pakistan had passed laws that made it illegal to leave Islam, punishable by death. Mom and Dad could clearly see this practice was not comparable to the loving invitation of Christianity. They saw Islam for what it was: intolerant, legalistic and violent. It was a religion that punished people in the name of God," Herman said.

More followed. "Two other irreconcilable areas became apparent. Christianity offered grace and an intimate relationship with absolute assurance of salvation. Islam was authoritarian, works related and with no assurance of salvation, except as a martyr. You just could not know if you had done enough, until you got to heaven and faced Allah. The clincher for my parents was the fact that Allah expected you to die for him whereas Christ died for us."

He finished with, "Once the veil was removed and true Islam was exposed, it was only a matter of time before my parents would leave it. Out of fear of the fundamentalists and their own families, they did not reveal they had become Christians until they had actually left Pakistan." Their fears were justified. Herman explained, "People in East Germany are routinely shot by the government when they try to escape from the Iron Curtain. But the reality in Pakistan was that if you tried to leave Islam, your own family would feel obligated to shoot you, as an 'honor killing.'"

"So you're saying that Muslims are a pretty blood thirsty bunch and shouldn't be trusted?" I wanted clarification.

"No! That's not the point!" Herman was emphatic. "By far the majority of people who call themselves Muslim, are peaceful, sincere, prayerful and loving, just like my parents. Either out of ignorance or misinterpretation of the Muslim Trilogy they simply are not practicing, true, Fundamental Islam.

"Let me explain it another way. Leroy, your Dad is a contractor and two of your brothers are in construction, right," he asked rhetorically?

I answered anyway. "Yea, Leonard has been a contractor and Leon has done a lot of carpentry."

He continued his illustration, "And they attend church regularly, are very involved in all church activities and are prayerful in every thing they do, correct?"

"Of course," I came back just a little testily.

"Well, let's say that one of them decided to begin 'flipping' houses. Of course he would complete his 'due diligence' to be sure he could make a profit. Then he buys a fixer-upper in a different town where the building code is not the same as Fullerton, but he did not realize a different code would be in effect. Then he went to work and did everything up to code for Fullerton but unknowingly it did not meet code for that city. Would you still believe he is a Christian," he asked?

"My family wouldn't do that! They are smarter than that! And besides, it would have been an honest mistake." I retorted, almost to the point of anger.

"Exactly, and don't get so defensive. It's all, hypothetical. But you would agree that the property really didn't meet code, right," he continued his thought?

Still a little touchy over the whole idea, I conceded, "Well, I guess not, but what does your 'situation' have to do with my questions?"

Herman leaned backed to study me more carefully. "Leroy, I believe you are familiar with the Gutenberg Printing Press and Martin Luther. And you are probably aware that up until the 1450s and 1500s, literacy was a luxury available only to the wealthy, as a rule. Up until then, most people could not read the Bible for themselves. And even if they could read, the Bible was almost always written in Latin. The printing press and Luther's drive to translate the Bible into the common language were two of the most significant things that resulted in a dramatic improvement in literacy and making the Bible accessible to the common people. This made it possible for the masses to know what was in the 'code' and the practice of indulgences was exposed for the usury it had been. It was now possible to have a direct advocacy with Jesus. Intercession was not a requirement as they had been duped into believing, not with a priest or even Mother Mary. You see, until they knew for themselves what was really in the Bible (the code), out of ignorance, they were practicing a religion that really didn't exist, much like your family practiced a 'code' that really didn't exist in that particular town. What you don't know really can hurt you."

He continued to elaborate. "Islam experienced something very similar but with the opposite results. The Muslim world has had a very large illiteracy problem for hundreds of years. Remember, Muhammad was illiterate himself. When the Koran was finally written down, it was written in Arabic and roughly 85% or more of all Muslims cannot read it. They have to depend on their Imams for interpretation, which leaves them vulnerable to the exact same issues facing early, illiterate Christians. For decades they have been told, by people such as Sayyid Qutb, a radical Egyptian hero to Muslims and Godfather to the Muslim Brotherhood, they must participate in violent Jihad. 'Jihad must be carried out in all countries that do not obey Sharia law:'[21] You simply aren't a true Muslim unless you are radical. Jihad is mandatory (Koran 9:39). That is why I believe the majority of people who identify as Muslims are practicing a religion that simply does not exist. Unfortunately, millions of people do just that, either by a decision or by default. And in spite of the fact that only about 15% of the Muslims in the world, are truly "fundamental-ists," the silence and deference of the rest of them help to con-tinue the myth that Islam is a peaceful religion," he concluded.

My response was almost a question, "I think I see your point." But I was less than 100% convinced. Still confused and not com-pletely up to speed on Herman's reasoning, I resigned myself to the goal I would some time in the future, study up on all he had given me. For now, my brain was pretty much fried and needed a change of subject.

Now What?

"For I know the plans that I have for you," declares
the Lord, "plans for welfare and not for calamity
to give you a future and a hope." (Jer. 29:11)

Herman would have been very comfortable as a Lutheran minister. Reyhadi lectures always had three parts to them and today he didn't waver from that formula. He always started out with some kind of bad news or the description of a 'problem' (my nominal faith). Then he would explain various options that were open to the listener (memorize scripture). Then he would scoop you up from any depression or confusion and give you some good news. Today he had something special to tack on at the end.

"I really didn't mean to blast you out of the water, but I figured this might be my last chance to let you see yourself the way others do and more importantly, how God sees you. I tried to answer your questions, but I don't want to just tell you what I believe and leave it at that. I am really hoping that some of this advice sticks. It will help you so much more to answer some of those questions for yourself." In the spirit of the moment, I was nodding my head. I truly intended to get to work on my own faith journey. Faith journey! It sounded adventurous and doable.

He wasn't finished. "I have some good news and I think you will be pretty excited. But first let me make some predictions. Your track career is going to take off and you will start getting better grades as well."

"How do you know that?" I wondered.

"Simple. There are three things that confirm this. First, I have been praying for you to blossom on the track and in the classroom. Second, you are young for your class. You just turned eighteen a few days ago (July 22) and with another year of maturation you will probably improve dramatically. You took third in the State Mile, running against athletes one and two years older than you. It is logical that you will catch up physically. Third, and this is the good news, I overheard De Groot (assistant Track Coach) and Tucker (Head Football Coach) talking to Coach Bush (Head Track Coach). It isn't official yet, and no one is supposed to know, but Bush has been hired to take over the FJC Track and Cross Country programs. He is sure to build them up, just the way he did here at the high school. In his short time at Fullerton he has already brought our program up out of the doldrums with two league championships in Track and one in Cross Country. And he knows you like a book and will bring you along very fast and I mean fast in both ways."

Dumbfounded, I just sat there with my mouth open. It was too much to take in. I had been dreading joining the FJC Track and Cross Country programs. They were near the bottom of the Eastern Conference in Track and had trouble even fielding a team in Cross Country. Bush had been like a father to my older brother. Their relationship went back to before I entered high school. He had coached Leon who had won the CIF, regional meet and then went to the State Meet in Chico in 1956 and placed second. Over the years he had been to our house a number of times. But a particularly poignant event happened sometime earlier.

Two years before high school (try the 7th grade) Bush had a summer job at the high school swimming pool. On a particularly warm day I had gone to the pool and then inexplicably, stole money from four or five of the lockers with the intention of buying myself something to eat. Like most kids caught in something bad, I could give no sane reason for this act. Even worse, was the fact that my parents owned a restaurant only five blocks South on Spadra (four blocks South of Buddy's) where food was free on demand. No matter, Bush caught me. After a short ride in a police cruiser to that same restaurant and a loud chewing out by my father I hoped it was all over.

Two years later, when I got to high school Leon drug me out to join him and Leonard (my other older brother) on the Cross Country team in the Fall of 1955 (see Appendix A, 2). There stood Coach Jim Bush with his clipboard taking names. I was terrified that he would remember. He never did but I spent the next eight years doing everything he asked, immediately and with out question. I was compliant to the point of being a mind-numbed little robot out of fear that at any time he would suddenly remember the "dirty little thief." And so, after a somewhat successful high school career, I joined him at FJC for two phenomenal years. What ever he said, to me it was gospel. Virtually joined at the hip, we then matriculated to Occidental College for another two years. Our eight-year conjoined careers paid off in spades. We had a lot of crazy success together but most important was his influence on building my character. He always gave God credit for his successes and he set a rigid example of honesty and hard work ethics while holding his athletes accountable for their behavior as well as any success. Jim Bush was responsible for my athletic successes and any strength of character traits I developed more than any other individual in my life. At the time I did not understand the magnitude of his influence. Looking in the rear view mirror, it was absolutely monumental. Whereas Herman's influence was by logic and revelation, Bush's effect on me was by his giant example. This prepared me to later accept what as yet I did not want to even consider.

For the moment, I needed to catch my breath. This was an unbelievable turn of events. "H-h-he is," I finally stammered? Herman confirmed that I had heard correctly. I didn't know if I should try to find my girlfriend and go somewhere special to celebrate or grab my training shoes for a work out. Suddenly, I felt invincible. FJC now sounded like a terrific option.

Chapter 2

TEN-YEAR REUNION

Catching Up

"For I long to see you so that I may impart some spiritual gift to you, that you may be established; that is, that I may be encouraged together with you while among you, each of us by the other's faith, both yours and mine." (Romans 1:11–12)

Saturday, October 4, 1969, 8:30 PM, San Antonio Hotel, Norwalk, California: The FUHS ten-year reunion is in full swing. If there is one thing common with most ten-year reunions it would be the vanity on display. Solomon and his verses in Ecclesiastes would have felt very much at home ("all is vanity and striving after the wind"). I however, felt very uncomfortable.

Everyone there seemed to be fully launched into eloquent and gaudy careers of fulfillment and riches. And apparently there was some sort of competition going on comparing careers and clothes. A number of them were already well into their second or even third marriages. Me? I had yet to have a fulltime job, let alone a career or even get married. I had mustered out of the Marine Corps in November of 1968 after returning from Viet Nam and used my GI (Government Issue) benefits to register at San Diego State University to begin working on a Graduate Degree in the Spring semester of 1969. At the reunion I now had one and a half semesters of classes under my belt. All alone, I kept scanning the room for Herman and his wife Cindy. I needed someone to hang with. It was incredible how many people were there whom I had absolutely no clue as to who they were. Herman and Cindy would give me cover for a while but I assumed they would have plans with other couples so my visit with them was sure to be brief.

Waiting for them, my mind wandered back to Buddy's Burgers in 1959. I was still amazed at how Herman's predictions had come true and were fulfilled ten times over. I had passed "Dumbbell English" and became a Business Major at FJC. My grades zoomed up to 2.36! And just as he predicted, my Track and Cross Country career had become nothing short of breathtaking. At one of the largest track meets in the world, the Mt.

SAC Relays, our Sprint Relay won and set a National Junior College record. I anchored the team with my best time ever in the 880 yard run (half-mile). Then in Modesto, in May I won the California State 880, setting a new individual National Record.

One year later I ran on five different relay teams that broke National Records a combined nine times. When we returned to Modesto for the 1961 State Championship, I won the Mile in a State Record, missing the National Record by .1 seconds (see Appendix A-3). I then took second in the 880, beating my previous year's time and finished the night with a 48.4 leg on the Mile Relay. Our Relay team won and set a new State Meet Record.

Just as Herman had predicted, Bush had turned the FJC program completely around. It was similar to flushing a toilet. Out with the old and in with the new. In his very first year the Fullerton Hornets won the Eastern Conference Track Championship for their first team title in recent memory. Then in 1960–61, we won the conference Cross Country title and repeated as conference Track Team champions. At the State Meet in Modesto we scored 50 points to win the team title there also.

After the official season was over, I competed in the 1500 meter run at the Southern Pacific Amateur Athletic Union Championship. It featured Junior College, University and club runners from Nevada, Arizona and California. In an Olympic year, it would have been a qualifying meet to try out for the USA Team. I won with a time of 3:48.9 (about a 4:07 Mile). Ducky Drake, the head track coach at UCLA was in the stands and offered me a "Full Ride" scholarship. I wasn't quite ready to commit because USC wanted me to visit their campus with the same "Full Ride" offer. Ridding high I was pretty full of myself. The Golden Boy could do no wrong.

In the summer of 1961, I finally decided I would go to UCLA. However, a few weeks before classes were to start I was jolted out of my socks. Coach Bush had been hired as the new Track Coach at Occidental College and wanted to know if I was interested in joining him there. Once again we were reunited. I had a terrific career at OXY with a number of first place points against UCLA (see Appendix A, 4), Arizona State, Arizona University and a few other Universities plus running on some winning relay teams, including a first place finish in the Two Mile Relay at the Coliseum Relays in 1963. I managed to win the open mile at the Mt. SAC Relays and then set the school record in the Mile at 4.05.4. After graduation, with a 2.2 GPA in Physical Education (OXY would only accept me if I changed my Major), I joined the Marine Corps. And now, having completed my three-year hitch, I was more than happy to be back in school. I had a totally new outlook on life and especially education.

Back at the reunion I heard my name being called from across the ballroom floor. It was Herman, finally. "Where have you been," I demanded, as he came over and gave me a bear hug! "Hey, where is Cindy," I wanted to know?

"She couldn't come, so it's you and me again, just like old times," Herman grinned.

We shuffled off into a quiet corner to catch up on each other. A lot of incredible things had happened to me since our lunchtime meeting back at Buddy's and I was very curious about Herman's take on them. But first we had to catch up on each other's lives.

Herman filled me in on how he had graduated from Princeton and then went to Harvard Law School. He then went to Washington, D.C. where he joined a big law firm and began to have a lot of success representing some pretty important people including a few Senators, a couple of professional athletes and some prominent media personalities. He had even argued a few cases before the Supreme Court with a 50/50 record of success. I filled him in on what I had been doing other than my track career, which he had kept up on, all along. I then caught him up on Viet Nam and my academic heroics in Graduate School.

What's Wrong with Those Jesus People?

"Every word of God is flawless; he is a shield to those who take refuge in Him. Do not add to His words . . ." (Proverbs 30:5–6)

Once caught up we took a breather and downed a couple of beers while we looked around to see who was doing what. Nothing unusual or interesting caught our attention and I began to focus on how to ask Herman about an incident on campus. I was sure he would have some kind of answer to excuse what happened, but I felt a little uneasy about bringing it up because his answer might be one that I really didn't want to hear. In August I had enrolled in some Exercise Physiology classes and labs and was actually doing well enough, to the point I had begun to feel somewhat intellectually superior. I was getting straight A's and undergraduates were coming to me for help in their lab assignments. I was feeling pretty smart and didn't need a moral compass or accountability lectures. I had been dating Ellen a pretty young lady in one of my lab classes. She was very bright and an atheist. We did what pleased us and no one got hurt, so there was no need for religion to get in the way. At twenty-eight years old I was completely satisfied with myself. I was superman.

One day Ellen came into the lab with a big grin on her face. I asked what was up. She said me she had been confronted by some Jesus-People up at the Student Union. They had argued with her for an hour trying to convince her Jesus was the answer to all her problems. They claimed that science and Christianity were not at odds with each other and advised her where she should want to end up in eternity. They wanted her to acknowledge her sins, ask for forgiveness and begin a new life of joy and freedom. Finally, the young lady who had taken the lead in talking to Ellen became exasperated, stomped her foot and growled through clinched teeth, "What is it about you intellectuals that you are the hardest to convince?" To which Ellen replied, "I think you just answered your own question, sweetie!"

Back at the lab we shared a hearty laugh over the incident, but, although I had given Ellen a pat on the back for her quick thinking, I was uneasy about the incident and needed Herman's input.

"So Herman, are you still all warm and fuzzy about Jesus?" His look told me that it was a dumb question so I explained the incident to him and asked what he thought about it. I was convinced he would have trouble with this one and was looking forward to a "gotcha" moment. The Jesus-People had totally blown it with Ellen. They had not come close to cracking her intellectual armor. In fact, they had been discredited, big time!

Typical of Herman, he did not immediately launch into his answer. He listened while staring into the distance then turned his attention to me. He grinned then quietly and deftly skewered me, "Leroy, you just tried to set me up! You and your friend felt pretty superior and in control, didn't you!"

Once again, in a few words he had cut my legs out from under me. "OK, OK, I admit I thought this one would be hard for you to explain. But I really do want your thoughts about the incident. I can't put my finger on it but for some reason I have been uneasy about how much I enjoyed the way it turned out? I don't understand why I felt so conflicted."

"Well, you are in luck," Herman smiled, "because I have some answers about how you felt and the confrontation itself.

"Leroy, I'm sure you would agree there are good teachers and bad teachers in all subjects. And there are undoubtedly good and bad track coaches. Parents, politicians, historians, railroad engineers can be good or bad, but in all cases, their lack of ability in no way invalidates the subject, wouldn't you agree?" I could already see where he was going. The Jesus-People who had challenged Ellen, were not very good at their job. It wasn't a weakness in the Gospel that had been exposed; it was their approach.

Herman continued to develop his answer, "If I had been the supervisor of that team, when they came back to be debriefed I

69

would have counseled them that they had lost sight of what their primary job was. The girl who 'lost it' forgot that her job was simply to proclaim the Gospel, not to wait around to see how successful she was. She did not need to add or subtract anything from the pure Gospel itself. It will stand on it's own. Sometimes we will see results right away but most of the time it is a process of planting a seed and then turning it over to the Holy Spirit. We will frequently be disappointed if we try to keep score."

His next offering scared the bejeebers out of me. "Leroy, I think I know why you felt conflicted. You are starting to have a conscience. You have begun to realize that you are a sinner and in need of forgiveness. I think God is calling you and you are starting to listen. In your heart you knew that Ellen's 'victory' was a hollow one." Stunned, I sat there with my mouth open to speak but nothing came out. I felt like the only naked person in the room.

Herman finally broke the ice for me. "I can't tell you how many times I have run into a wall, realizing how sinful I am. At those times I have felt totally exposed and vulnerable. But soon after I regain my balance and feel completely energized. Forgiven!" His talk brought me back to the present. I felt scared but kind of glad it had happened. I mumbled something in the order of thanks or I needed that. Perhaps those seeds were starting to sprout.

The Jesus-People event had been a stall. I really wanted to ask about something much more serious. But I continued with questions about lesser things for the moment.

That's Just Not Right

"For He causes His sun to rise on the evil and the good, and sends the rain on the righteous and the unrighteous." (Matthew 5:45)

"Herman, there are some other things I need your take on." I did a little tap dance around what really had me on edge. "Remember our talk about Christianity back at Buddy's?" I asked.

"Spit it out! What is this all about?" he came back with a slight grin. He had always enjoyed toying with me when I wasn't sure of myself.

"Well, I guess it's my turn to ask something from out of left field. I've been noticing a lot of things in the news, I've been to 'Nam and saw a lot of bad stuff, there's a lot of talk about abortion and there seems to be a lot of violence in the world that just doesn't make sense. Is it me or do you think there has been a world wide shift in values to the point that human life simply isn't worth that much anymore?" I asked, trying to sound informed and objective.

"Wow!" Herman exclaimed. "You didn't just come to town and fall off the turnip truck, did you! What were they feeding you in the Marine Corps? You have become a serious person!"

"Well, like I said, I have noticed some things that have me wondering how a theologian like yourself might explain them," I couldn't help but return the prick. "There is just something weird about the JFK assassination on the same day that C.S. Lewis and Aldous Huxley died. Was that a coincidence or some kind of prophetic statement," I was sincerely asking? "Also, there are reports about Malcom X being assassinated by some radical Muslims and there were the Watts riots, the Mai Lai massacre in 'Nam and the Tate/La Bianca murders by the Manson family. It's just nuts out there. When we went to grammar school and high school, I don't remember it being so bad. Has the world changed that much or are we just now becoming aware of it? Is this what we should expect from now on?"

Herman thought for a moment before he began his careful answer. "First you need to have a little perspective on those things. Remember the newspaper adage that 'blood sells.' I know that it seems like there is nothing but violence out there but a lot of very positive things have happened too. JFK started the Peace Corps, which is doing a lot of good things in other countries. Neil Armstrong stepped on the moon. And over in South Africa, Dr. Barnard has been successful with heart transplants. Schools here in the US have been integrated and the World Trade Center in New York is quite a success story. Even in Track and field, look at all the world records that have been broken in just the last few years, three of them at the Olympics in Mexico City." Then he chided me with, "And of course your man Nixon won the election, which really hurts because I voted for Humphrey."

I agreed that a few good things had happened. But my real question was, "How can a good and omnipotent God allow so much evil to persist?"

He sobered up and was serious again, "Leroy, we live in a sinful and imperfect world. Oddly enough, this can be thought of as a good thing because it gives us the liberating option of 'free choice.' As all-powerful as God is, he will not run our lives as if we don't have a mind and a will of our own. That's why understanding Matthew 5:44–48 is key to what our outlook on life should be. He is not going to drag you kicking and screaming into heaven. He wants your love, given freely, not coerced obedience like what you see in Islam.

"Once you recognize and acknowledge that you cannot do anything of your own power He will immediately send the Holy Spirit to dwell inside you and enable you to confess your sins and follow Him. 'For it is by Grace you have been saved, through faith—and this not from yourselves, it is the gift of God—not by works, so that no one can boast.' (Ephesians 2:8)

I mumbled something about how that made sense but my mind was actually on something else. I finally got my nerve up to ask the big question, the one that was really troubling me. "Do you think God has a plan for me?"

"Holy crap!" he cried in amazement. "Why do you ask that?"

The floodgates opened up and I began to pour out the details that had me questioning where I had been, where I might be going and about life in general. A few incidents in Viet Nam had me a little shaken up and confused. For me, life had always been taken for granted. My success as an athlete had trained me to believe that no matter what happened, I would land on my feet and things would be nothing but fun and games again. But some of those events in Viet Nam could not be easily explained away. "Herman, how do you know if Jesus or God is watching over you? I mean, does He, Them, the both of Them and I suppose the Holy Spirit too, have a plan for my life?"

"Absolutely," he retorted forcefully!

I filled him in on one particular incident that had me wondering how I had come back from Viet Nam in one piece while
so many others, seemingly with so much more to return to than
myself, came back in body bags. It happened just outside Da
Nang. I had been billeted temporarily in an Eli (Eelee) hut (ply-
wood floors, tin roof and wire mesh walls) located about thirty
feet from the double rows of spiraling concertina wire that surrounded and protected our compound, while my unit waited for
another outfit to leave so we could take their place. I slept in the
North East corner of that hut for only three nights. When the other
outfit finally pulled out I moved into a different hut about fifty
yards up the hill. Another officer took my original place. That
night the Viet Cong attacked our compound and broke through
the wire next to the hut I had slept in the night before. A satchel
charge (athletic bag full of explosives and shrapnel) was thrown
into the hut and the officer who had taken my place was killed
by the explosion (see Appendix A, 5). The fact that I had survived was inexplicable. I hadn't performed heroically or even
done anything noticeably above average. There was nothing in
my performance that indicated I was unusually important for the
completion of our mission. I wasn't spared because of any unique
contribution on my part. To this day, I carry pictures of the blown
up hut with shrapnel lodged in the rafters and blood on the floor

where I had slept the night before to remind myself how easily it could have been me coming home in a body bag. This providential act had to mean something significant but I didn't know what. Now, my question was, "Why was I spared?"

Herman bit his lip and shook his head, "That's a tough one."

Adding to my confusion, I confessed, "You know how much of a nominal, slacker I was in high school. But at least I went to church. However, after high school I quit going altogether. In fact, I became a real heathen. Long nights, cold beers and hot women became my M. O. In spite of that, I was spared. Why?"

Herman leaned into his answer. "It's not for me to give you an absolute and definitive answer. I can tell you that He causes the sun to shine and the rain to fall on the righteous and unrighteous alike. What this means is that Christians are not exempt from what happens in this sinful world. And you have to wrestle with this and decide for yourself what it means. No one can do it for you. However, I can help with the process. This is one of those situations where you need the right tools. Remember that? My first thought is that maybe God has something special He has saved you for. If you will just turn to Him, He will reveal it. Remember Jeremiah 29:11 back at Buddy's? 'For I know the plans I have for you,' declares the Lord, 'Plans for welfare and not for calamity to give you a future and a hope.' God was actually talking to Israel as a whole but it applies to you as an individual too. Matthew 7:7–12 would be a good place for you to start looking for answers," Herman counseled me.

"The main thing is you have to start praying for God to reveal what he wants you to do. Then you have to listen for the answers. God will most certainly find ways to tell you what He wants. But it will only come if you are sincerely seeking Him. I think God has been sending messages to you for a long time but you have shouted Him down with your self-absorption. Listen to that little voice inside you. It might be hard at first but if you keep trying, it will become easier and easier."

He then cautioned me, "But I must warn you that your being spared may not be a celestial message. The only way you are going to know whether God has something special in mind for you or that you simply got caught in the 'sunshine' is if you seek God with all you heart and all your soul."

His advice was helpful but I still had a stubborn streak in me that just wouldn't let me turn my life over to anyone (or God); however, I did intend to become an active listener. That wouldn't demand too much from me.

Partners Again

"Two are better than one because they have a good return for their labor. For if either of them falls, the one will lift up his companion. But woe to the one who falls when there is not another to lift him up." (Ecclesiastes 4:9,10)

As I wrestled with all Herman had just laid on me I noticed that he had become very quiet and was staring off into space. "I appreciate what you have just shared and I am going to think about it a lot," I promised then paused. "Hey, are you OK?" He came back to the present but the look on his face spoke volumes. Something bad was happening. "What's going on?" I demanded.

Herman cleared his throat but his voice cracked when he tried to speak. He closed his eyes for a moment and started over, "Hey, I'm sorry. Here I am this bastion of Christian manhood but all this talk about your questions has convicted me of some of my own problems," he said trailing off. "I'm giving you all this great advice but I'm drowning in guilt and self pity, myself. OK, you would find out sooner or later any way. Cindy and I have split up," he admitted, almost in tears.

"No way!" I protested. "What happened?" I cautiously asked, feeling his pain.

He began to explain, "Well, you know we got married my senior year at Princeton. And for about two years it was 'the best.' I have to take most of the blame because I got so wrapped up in law school that I began to neglect our marriage. I got worse when my career took off. I was hardly ever at home. I worked late and just kind of blew it! Money was never a problem but our sex life went south and we fought constantly. She finally had had enough and began the divorce stuff. I didn't fight it. I didn't even try marriage counseling. I was too much into my career and was sort of glad to be free again. Like I said, my faith has really been challenged. I am praying for forgiveness but there isn't any hope of us putting things back together.

"Leroy, I have a big favor to ask. I have decided to put my career on hold and take off a year or two. I need to get out of DC and away from all the things that drug me down. Since you're single and going to San Diego State, would you consider taking me in as a roommate?" he asked. "I've already lined up a job teaching Special Ed. classes over in the Grossmont School District and will certainly be able to pay my share of the rent. My thinking is that concentrating on helping those kids will be very humbling and good therapy."

It took me about five seconds to answer. "That would be fantastic! Just like old times! Partners again," I effused until I remembered what occasioned this turn of events. At twenty-eight years of age, I was still single with no prospects of marriage in sight. But something inside me, maybe it was that little voice Herman always talked about, had a reverence for the institution of marriage. Divorce, even for some one else, felt like a punch in the stomach. Who knew? Maybe there was hope for me after all?

Chapter 3

BELIEVE IT OR DON'T

Strawberry Waffles

Jesus answered, "It is written: 'Man does not live on bread alone, but on every word that proceeds out of the mouth of God'" (Matthew 4:4)

Sunday, October 22, 1969, 10:30AM, Carnation restaurant, East San Diego, California: After our ten-year reunion Herman took some time off from his career and moved in with me. While I attended classes at San Diego State he taught "Special Ed." at a high school in nearby La Mesa, beginning in January. In the mean time he did a lot of reading while I began getting back into shape by running up to ten and twelve miles per day. Perhaps polar opposites do attract. Herman certainly filled in as the Yin of my Yang. Most notable, we were still a long way apart spiritually. I was self-absorbed and constantly looking for personal gratification. I tended to use people. He was serious, interested in developing his intellectual gifts while broadening his perspectives. He was engaged with and respectful of others. However, slowly but surely I had begun to question everything about myself, my way of life and, very importantly, what if Herman was right about the hereafter. Was I really leading an immoral life that would eventually have consequences? Was Christianity everything he had always preached to me that it was? As I teetered between submission and hedonism, I worried, would I have to give up all the fun and freedom if I became a stoic, pew buster?

We discussed everything from "soup to nuts" at the drop of a hat but Sundays were special. Like clock work, after Herman came home from church, usually around 10:30 AM, we would walk around the apartment building to an alley that led to the parking lot of a Carnation restaurant, located on the next street over. It became a ritual to have a strawberry waffle with link sausages. Nothing serious was discussed until the last morsel had been consumed. Then we practically closed the place down, talking about the big stuff for hours. Now and then we lingered so long we ate dinner there also. Usually it began with one of my questions either out of sincere inquisitiveness or sometimes as a challenge to one of his positions.

Truth or Consequences

Pilate therefore said to Him, "So you are a king?"
Jesus answered, "You say correctly that I am a
king. For this I have been born, and for this I
came into the world, to bear witness to the truth.
Everyone who is of the truth hears My voice."
Pilate said to Him, "What is truth?" (John 18:37)

With over 25,000 students, San Diego State University was large and diverse. The West Commons (cafeteria & student center) where I hung out between classes had its share of pot-heads, nerds, studious commuters and foreign students. In that mix were a number of Saudis, Pakistanis and other middle-eastern students. Some happened to be the male offspring of rich oil barons. They let it be known they would pay top dollar for sexual indulgences and the price went up if the purveyor of those benefits were blond and blue eyed. My friend Ellen had been propositioned several times. On the other hand, a number of them appeared to be very serious about their education and did not act like they were on spring break at a beach in Florida. I almost never interacted with them but did observe a situation that pricked my curiosity and I made a mental note to grill Herman about it. That next Sunday after the last bite of waffle disappeared, I brought it up.

"I have to tell you about last week at the West Commons. I sat at a table next to one where two middle-eastern students were sitting. I assume they were Muslims because they were reading their Korans. A couple of American guys came over and sat down with them. They all seemed to know each other and apparently the American guys were doing research for a debate comparing the Bible to the Koran. I couldn't quite hear their specific questions but they seemed to be asking about the pros and cons of the two holy books. The Muslims said something about how the Bible was not dependable and that the Koran was God's last word for humans to live by and that it had never been altered. They claimed it was perfect but the Bible had a lot of errors in it."

The word "debate" gained Herman's full attention, "So what's your question?"

"Well, I was remembering all you told me about your parents and how they became Christians. It was very interesting but I don't remember you going into much detail about the Koran and especially how it stacks up against the Bible. I do remember you saying something about abrogation but you didn't say a whole lot more about it. How do we know which one is the truth?" I might just as well have thrown slop to the hogs. He dove in.

Once again he was way ahead of me. He smiled wryly, "I've been waiting a long time for that question. I wanted you to bring it up so you wouldn't feel manipulated."

My first thought was to blow him off. He didn't have to come off so superior. But I really was searching for answers so I brushed it off and asked for more.

He began with a reasoned approach. "First, lets spend just a minute or two looking at this comparison from a perspective of simple logic. Would you agree that the Old Testament is basically a story whereby God reveals Himself and His true nature while continuously pointing to the need for a sacrificial lamb, that is a Messiah, namely Jesus?"

"Sounds about right," I admitted.

He went on. "And would you agree that the New Testament is basically a fulfillment of Old Testament prophesy? And that it tells us all about Jesus and His life and how the apostles began to build the early church, with a few new prophecies and revelations thrown in?"

Again I had to more or less agree. I had not read the Bible enough to intelligently discuss such things.

"Good," he exclaimed! He then began to close the loop of his line of thought, "Now who wrote the Bible, when did they write it and did Jesus write any of it?"

I did recall some of this information, "I believe you said there were forty authors over a fifteen hundred year period. And no, Jesus did not write anything," I proudly responded. "Actually, although that is the most commonly accepted number and time span, there is some debate on the subject. Some sources say there were 35 authors and some say as many as 45. And the time frame ranges from 1200 years to 1800 years. Some of the confusion about the number of authors comes from the fact that some of the books were written by 'unknown' authors.[1,2] Someone wrote Joshua, Judges, Ruth and Hebrews and a few of the other books, but it is not exactly clear who it was by name. And the time line is a little jumbled because some of Genesis comes from an oral tradition that Moses wrote down hundreds of years later. But that's just a lot of minutia and doesn't need to concern us all that much." He then asked, "Who wrote the Koran and when was it written?"

Again I was quite pleased with myself, "Actually, Muhammad orally dictated it to his followers, over about twenty-three years and they wrote some of it down over time and it was finally collected into it's fully written form by about 630 to 650 AD, all about 250 years after the Bible."[3]

Herman couldn't help but grin a little, "So which story is the most believable? The one with forty independent writers over fifteen hundred years, all in agreement about someone else or the autobiography by one person about himself with no corroboration?" The simplicity of his argument was powerful.

"There are two more general points before we get into specifics. One big mistake that most people make in this comparison is they equate the Koran to the Bible. They assume the Koran fills the same roll for Islam as the Bible does for Christianity. That is not at all the case. For Christians the Bible is the story about God's relationship to mankind and the history of Christianity covering about 10,000 to 16,000 years, depending on your understanding of archaeology, Biblical genealogy, linguistics, DNA and so forth. Jesus is the culmination of that story. The Koran, however, Islam believes is a direct revelation, word for word, from Allah, through Muhammad. It is his understanding about God's plan for the lives of Muslims. It is not about Muhammad per se; he is merely the conduit. Essentially it is 'orders from headquarters' in that it is a long list of specific directives to Muslims to do certain things and not do other things.

"For Christians, the Bible is the anchor and primary source of inspiration and guidance with Jesus as the fulfillment of those teachings and prophecies. On the other hand, the Koran can be generally thought of as similar to a picture frame. It is sort of an outline with lots of directives and generalities. It serves as a guide for Islamic principles but it is only one third of the story of Islam. Muhammad provides more specific instructions by his examples because Muhammad IS Islam and Islam **IS** Muhammad. Thus the Koran can only be understood in the light of Muhammad's life (the Sira) and the precedents (the Hadith) he set. It is not an historical document like the Bible. Muhammad and Islam could survive without the Koran but the Koran could not survive without Muhammad. In fact, some Islamic scholars indicate that Islam is 10% Koran and 90% Hadith and Sira.[4] Jesus and the Bible are inseparable. They rise and fall together as one."

He expanded on the differences and similarities. "It's an important, but often overlooked point that what Muhammad really needed was a book of scripture for the Arabs. He obviously knew a lot about the Old Testament and repeatedly extolled the Injeel as the revealed word of God. But they were written in Hebrew and Greek thus practically useless to Muhammad's people. The Koran would give the Arab world an equivalent guidance system, in Arabic."

"Wait a minute," I pleaded, "are you saying that the Bible and the Koran are somewhat interchangeable but Jesus and Muhammad are not?"

"No and yes," came his simple reply. "But it gets pretty complicated," he added. "Islam believes that the Koran is the exact words of God, given to Muhammad, telling Muslims how to live and behave, like a manual for life but the Bible was written by men who were inspired by God to write their stuff down but they used their own words, feelings and thoughts. That is, it was not dictated by God. The one exception is they believe the Ten Commandments were literally, word for word, given to Moses from God. This is the reason so many of them go 'nuts' if the Koran is slighted in the least but are not at all disturbed if the Bible is smeared with feces or burned. To them one is Holy and must be fanatically defended and protected. The other is just the story of Christianity, a biography, if you will. But they both serve as a guide, one by interpreting its historical record and the other by its directives. And as to comparing Jesus to Muhammad, some Muslims see a closer connection between Mary and Muhammad than with Jesus."

"Say, what? Muhammad and Mary? Where do you get that idea?" I was aghast.

"Well now, just think about it. Both presumably were illiterate; both were visited by an angel; both were given an important mission; both then experienced a "miracle"; Mary became pregnant without 'knowing' a man and Muhammad produced the Koran and to Muslims, an illiterate man, producing the Koran is proof, in their eyes that a true miracle had taken place. At the same time, Islam truly believes in Jesus and his works, just not the crucifixion or that he was also God, in human form. They do not equate Jesus and Muhammad. They see them as two separate prophets, chosen by God for distinct and separate missions, but Muhammad was superior to Jesus, because he brought God's (Allah's) final revelation.

"Another mistake by many people, including Christians, is that they look at the Bible as mostly an historical document. To them, it is all about something in the past. Nowhere is this more evident than in the case of miracles. Modern day miracles are generally not believed or at least people are more skeptical of them than the historical ones. This too is a big mistake. If you can believe in the Creation, why not modern miracles which would be infinitely less taxing on an all-powerful God than His Creation. If you think of the Bible as a communication system from God about the past, the present and the future, you will be far ahead in understanding how incredible it really is.

"Now I want to focus on a more objective approach and set this up so anyone can understand and it will be easy to remember," he began to flesh out his method. Herman never approached any problem or challenge in a haphazard or piece-meal fashion. If nothing else, he was systematic and thorough. Even the way he ate was methodical. First he ate all the peas, then he would rotate his plate and eat all the mashed potatoes and concluded his ritual with one more rotation to finish off the roast beef. "Most Muslims will sound very much alike because their memorized arguments have been spoon fed to them by their Imams and each other. Very few of them have actually studied original material in the Bible or the Koran to come up with those arguments. In fact, most of them (80–85% +/-) can't even read the Koran in the original Arabic for themselves yet they claim that any translation will totally lose the original meaning. We want to avoid their errors so we need to be as methodical and objective as we can. Let's start by deciding how we can evaluate the two books with equal scrutiny and see what happens," he ambled on as if I wasn't there.

Herman was always so thorough getting his ducks in a row the listener almost never had to participate. "Let's compare both of them against just four constructs." Whether you were Muslim, Jew, or Atheist, who could derail this line of reasoning? Once in motion, Herman's powers of persuasion were daunting. He continued to build his evaluation grid with, "Let's say that Construct #1 is Unity, #2 is Prophecy, #3 is Inerrancy and #4 is Understandability." My head had already started to ache. He rolled happily on.

Next he cleverly preempted the basic strategy of some of the more popular Muslim arguments, "Let's think for just a minute about what we might see after we go through these steps. It would be normal to expect that the book which took the longest to write, with input from a dramatically greater number of contributors and had been around hundreds of years longer, is the most likely to fail cross examination by these constructs because of the multitude of opportunities to break down, wouldn't you agree?"

"Well, I'm not really sure," I mumbled. He had set his trap. I could see where he was headed but it was baffling to me how he could get there. "OK, for the sake of your precious constructs, I will say that I agree," I patronized. What else could I say without coming up with my own method to compare the two holy books?

"Terrific," he chirped gleefully. One of my pet peeves was how he always took such pleasure in letting you know he was an expert in something you were completely in the dark on and then rubbing it in. DANG! But once he let you in on what he knew, you would immediately forgive him because it was invariably quite valuable. "Well, in fact the opposite is true," he said as he finished the set up. "No other book in the history of the world has withstood the test of time and attacks by its enemies like the Bible has," he declared. To underscore his position, he then quoted from a book by some guy named Bernard Ramm. "No other book has been so chopped, knived, sifted, scrutinized and vilified. What book on philosophy or religion or psychology or *belles lettres* of classical or modern times has been subject to such a mass-attack as the Bible?"[5]

"Yet it has survived and flourished," bubbled Herman.

Construct #1
UNITY

"The glory that You have given Me I have given to them; that they may be one, just as We are one; I in them and Thou in Me, that they may be perfected in unity, that the world may know that Thou didst send Me, and didst love them, even as Thou didst love Me." (John 17:22–23)

"One of the most amazing things to me about the Bible is its unity. Against all odds it is a harmonious story that time and again tells us about God's true nature while also showcasing human nature. It reveals our need for forgiveness and God's desire to forgive. It is a complete story with a continuous thread of prophecy and revelation. Key is the progressive nature of its prophecies beginning in Genesis and building to its fulfillment in the New

Testament. In spite of the diversity of writers and writing styles it tells one story. Over 1500 years in the making, the message rock solidly always points to the coming Messiah and His mission here on earth and then tells us God's plan to bring everything to a conclusion, in Revelation. Every book builds on the previous one and predicts events in later books." Herman was on autopilot as he gushed on about one of his favorite subjects.

"For instance, lets consider one of the many themes in the Old Testament, the need for a heartfelt offering out of obedience to please God. It began when Cain and Abel brought their sacrifices to God's alter. God was pleased with Abel's but rejected Cain's, possibly because he did it begrudgingly or perhaps it was not an acceptable sacrifice on his part. It is not totally clear why, but it is certain that God did reject his sacrifice for presumably, a very good reason. Then there's the story of Abraham and Isaac and we know how that went with a substitute for the sacrifice being provided when God was testing Abraham's obedience (Genesis 22:7–12). Of course we have to include the Passover Lamb as another example of God's need for a 'substitute' to pay for sin, with the Israelites obediently putting the blood of lambs on their door lintels as they were commanded. There are hundreds of examples in the Old Testament that lead us directly to Jesus on the cross as our sacrificial lamb," Herman was emphatic! "That was the ultimate example of obedience!

"Miracles also provide a unifying theme of the Bible," he said, picking up another thread of rationale. "They occur regularly throughout both the Old and New Testament. And in every case they convey a message or proof from God that He is real, that He is omnipotent and that He loves His Creation. We can begin with Creation itself and then consider the Flood. Then we can look at the plagues in Egypt, Moses holding back the water of the Red Sea, his striking a rock to get water, the provision of manna, the story of Joshua at Jericho, how Samson slew 1,000 Philistines with the jaw bone of a donkey and how David killed Goliath. I mean, there are so many it is hard to do justice to all of them," Herman was on the verge of stammering at the volume of miracles he was trying to describe.

"Of course, the miracles by Jesus are the most famous and commonly known by skeptics as well as Christians. He healed lepers, produced wine from water, raised dead people back to life and fed thousands with just a few fish and loaves. The pattern of miracles is inescapable and central to the unified messages of the Bible. In every case the miracle provides proof that God is all-powerful and encourages us to believe in Him and to be faithful," he concluded.

"Now, lets take a look at unity in the Koran," Herman ambled on. "I assume that you haven't read the Koran, correct?"

"Of course not. Why would I?" came my snippy reply.

He was just warming up, "Well, I have and I can to tell you it is a difficult book to read. It is similar to the Bible, in that there is a lot of stuff in it that is intended to reveal God's nature or Allah's nature, if you will. Strangely though, Muhammad and his role as Allah's messenger is not mentioned all that often, probably less than a dozen times but indirectly he is referred to as The Prophet all over the place.

"The Koran, by comparison, we would expect to exude continuity. It was written, or should we say, dictated by one man. Albeit, he did so over twenty-three years, the one-man authorship is part and parcel of the opportunity for a rock solid unified message. And, if as Muslims claim, it was a book inspired by Allah, it should absolutely be a clear, concise, convincing and unified message. But it is none of these," said Herman. "Rather it is a rambling, disconnected, often unclear series of statements surrounded by flowery rhetoric. Except for the story of Joseph there is no beginning, middle or end. There is no unity other than it's repeated admonitions of many rituals and works related activities required of every Muslim and that the Jews and Christians had polluted the Book (Bible), and the only guaranteed way to get to heaven is to die for Allah.

"Right from the start, the Koran contradicts itself as to whether Muhammad was or was not a prophet. In Surah's 6:50, 41:43 and 46:8, he admits that he was only sent to warn Christians and Jews of their errors and he did not claim to be a true prophet at that time. His wife finally convinced him that he was a prophet and eventually he came to believe in this calling and appeared to desire acceptance as a prophet by the early Christians. When they rejected him, he took his ball and went home to build his own version of faith in one God and only one.

Dozens and dozens of times in the Koran Muhammad points out how the people of the Book were in error and that he had the proper interpretation of God's will. He never set out to replace the Bible but to simply proclaim his addendum to it and to show how it was being abused. Modern Muslims claim many errors in the Bible but that position is not found in the Koran itself. In fact, although modern Muslims reject the Gospels as corrupt, the Koran itself commands them to read the Injeel as true revelation. His problem was rather he believed the Jews and Christians had bastardized it. The polytheism around him and the Christian's insistence on sinning against God, sickened him to the point of becoming a brutal fundamentalist.

"As another example of the lack of unity in the Koran," Herman continued to explain, "you need only to examine what it tells us about the creation of man. In the Bible we read that man was created from dust. Not to be outdone, Surah 15:26 tells us 'We created man of dried clay, of dark loam molded." But then in Surah 16:5, suddenly we are told, "Man hath he created from a moist germ (sperm)." Adding to the controversy, Surah 19:65 says, 'We come not down from heaven but by the Lord's command,' that is He spoke and we 'were.' Then in Surahs 21:31 and 24:44 the reader is told that all things were created from water. Further adding to the confusion, in 96:2, depending on which Hadith your read for interpretation, we are told that man was created from a clot of congealed blood or a 'hanging thing.' The angel Gabriel is credited with giving Muhammad all his visions. Unfortunately, when telling him about the creation of man, he was all over the parking lot with how it was, specifically accomplished. There is no unified message.

"There is another important difference between the Koran and the Bible when discussing unity," Herman continued his argument. "Notice that all Biblical references are written by eye witnesses to arguably historical events. These events and facts are pretty much confirmed by outside evidence. None of these events are contradictory; rather they build on each other. They all demonstrate the common thread of God giving a blessing, the Israelites enjoying a period of prosperity and then falling into sin followed by a time of hardship as God disciplines them and then they remember their God and return to Him. These events are often corroborated by well-known and respected extra-Biblical historians. And then it starts all over. It is a carbon copy of our own lives to day.

"The Koran, however, is based on one man's professed receiving of the 'words' of Allah from an angel. There are no other witnesses. There are no provable, historical aspects to this spelunker's accounts of his visions. It is true that when he leaves the cave where he received his visions, he then tells others about those visions, usually his wife or other close followers. But almost without exception, no one shares his experiences.

"Many historical events are found throughout the Koran itself, but they are limited to what Muhammad himself could have seen and more often than not, they are simply reworded accounts of Biblical references. On the other hand, the events in the Bible occur over thousands of years and are reported by multiple witnesses (many non-Jewish and non-Christian), often prophesied and later fulfilled.

"As I have already said, the story of Islam does provide some unity in that it is works related. Muslims are told many things to avoid, tons of things they must do and continually reminded of the honor it is to die for Allah. And they must perform up to a very high standard, much of it ritualistic such as praying five times a day (the Koran actually says to pray three times a day; five times a day comes from Muhammad's example) while facing Mecca. But even the direction of the prayers changed. Originally, they were to face toward Jerusalem when they prayed. Somewhere along the way, Mecca became the preferred direction, probably in an attempt to downplay any Jewish influence and/or to honor Muhammad.

"And unfortunately there is no provision for grading their performances. They are kept totally in the dark until they meet Allah in heaven, at which time it will be too late to make up for any short comings," said Herman. "In essence, unity in the Koran is simply to obey orders rather than an example of integrated literature. In reality, Islam is a phenomenon of 'group think.' Muslims are reminded over and over again that their unity is as a body of believers and that they must sacrifice everything for the group. Christians are members of a group of believers also, but their loyalty is to Christ.

"Islam also claims there are many miracles in the Koran that prove Muhammad knew what he was talking about and that the Koran was God's last word. Koranic miracles are purportedly, evidence of a unified message from Allah. Some are supposed to be scientific evidence. Some are just silly. One popular Muslim notion of scientific proof is basic numerology nonsense. They claim mathematical patterns in the Koran are 'miraculous' evidence that only God could have provided. There's just one problem with their complicated patterns of numbers. Those same numbers can be found, 'in the Bible, in the works of Edgar Allan Poe, and even in online message boards.'[6]

"They also claim that the basics of human reproduction were revealed in the Koran hundreds of years before medical science confirmed them as proof of another supposed miracle. Surah 23:13–14 states, "Then we made him a sperm in a fixed lodging, then we made the sperm into a hanging thing, then we made the hanging thing into a chewed thing, then we made the chewed thing into bones, then we clothed the bones with flesh, then we developed it into another creation, blessed be Allah, the best of creators." **Burrrrrrt! Wrong!** This flies in the face of basic Developmental Biology. The mesoderm differentiates into bone and flesh at the same time.[7] And the list goes on and on.

"The Koran contradicts itself in many other areas. I have already told you about abrogation. This process was invented by Muhammad to settle disputes over Koranic verses that seemed to be in direct conflict. It was his way of emphasizing which verse took precedence. The most obvious example is the one I told you about before, the one my parents latched onto. The Koran states, 'There is no compulsion with religion' only to reverse course and then say 'Kill them where you find them (infidels).' It is a false argument that the Koran is a unified message from Allah. Why would a perfect God have to change His story, which Allah does many times?"

The information was coming at me at warp speed. It felt like I was trying to take a drink from a fire hydrant. "Herman, slow down! I asked a few simple questions and you are giving me the Encyclopedia Britannica. Is there anyway you can answer my questions without the PhD. Dissertation?"

Herman stared at me for a moment then grinned. "Ok. I'll try to boil it down. He then moved on with a little dig, "Now let's take a look at Construct #2, Prophecy … from a grade school perspective."

I resigned myself to trying to get the big picture while ignoring details. Hopefully he would slow down as I expected this one would be more difficult to prove. He didn't even hesitate. It was 'Onward, Christian Soldiers.'

Construct #2

PROPHECY

"From now on I (Jesus) am telling you before it comes to pass, so that when it does occur you may believe that I am He." (John 13:19)

Herman began by making an important distinction. "Most people do not understand there are really two categories of prophecy. The one usually thought of is predictive prophecy. That is, someone, usually a recognized religious leader, or prophet, if you will, makes a statement about God's plans and that prediction eventually occurs. But another very important type is where a prophet speaks on God's behalf to advise, chastise, correct, inform or encourage someone, often a king or queen, military leader or some other servant of God. And sometimes there was no prophet at all. In Genesis, God often spoke directly to the person, telling them what was about to happen or what He wanted them to do and those events are considered prophecy as well. We will only look at the first one, and briefly at that so you won't be overwhelmed."

Excitedly, I piped in, "I think I know one of those. My Gramma Morefield used to tell us kids different stories from the Bible on her flannel board. One of my favorites was about Joseph and his many-colored coat." I was beaming as I recalled my grandmother's stories. "I remember her telling us how his brothers sold Joseph into slavery and along with a famine, that led to the Israelites eventually ending up in Egypt. All of that was prophesied in Genesis when God told Abraham that his offspring would be sojourners in a land that wasn't theirs and they would become servants, for four hundred years (Gen. 15:13–16)."

Herman just sat there with a bemused smile.

"What?" I demanded. "Why the big grin? I'm right ain't I?"

He enjoyed my consternation for a moment then explained. "Oh, you just reminded me of Proverbs 22:6, 'Train up a child in the way he is to go, even when he is old he will not depart from it,' he demurred. Leroy, as hard as you try to hide from God and as hedonistic as you try to be you simply can't escape Him. His messages have been planted inside you and it is only a matter of time before you will have to give up and give in! Your grandmother's stories are part of who you are!"

For a moment I was embarrassed and a little red-faced. He had caught me being excited and enthusiastic about the scriptures. I had to admit to myself, if no one else, those flannel board stories were some of my most cherished childhood memories. They reminded me of a time of innocence and the acceptance of Jesus as a matter of fact. Life was a lot easier in those days. "Aw, shut up," I scowled!

"OK, OK," he chortled. "Don't get all worked up over it." He returned to his prophecy theme. "One of Islam's biggest problems with Christians is their insistence on the prophecy of Jesus as the one and only Messiah and belief that He was who He said He was, namely God and man, and that He was prophesied many times in the Old Testament. I won't go into a lot of detail, but Muslims claim that most of those prophecies were about Muhammad. I will only explain two of them, to save time.

"Deuteronomy 18:18 is one of their (Muslims) favorites, where God tells Moses, 'I will raise up a Prophet from among their countrymen like you, and I will put My words in His mouth and He shall speak to them all that I command Him.' In Surah 7:157, Allah tells Muhammad, 'Say to them: O men! Verily, I am God's apostle to you all; therefore believeth on God and his Apostle-the unlettered prophet (the illiterate one) ... and follow him that ye may be guided aright.' Islam teaches that this is proof that Biblical scripture prophesied Muhammad. But that is all a bunch of baloney. The term 'countrymen' is the same as 'brethren,' namely the Jews or Israelites exclusively. God said he would raise up a prophet for the Levites from among 'their brethren,' that is, from one of the other tribes of Israel." Muhammad was an Ishmaelite (Arab), not from any of the tribes of Israel.[8]

"On the other hand, Jesus fulfilled the prophecy perfectly. First, He was of the 'Line of David.' He was an Israelite from one of the twelve tribes and therefore one of the 'brethren.' You can also add on all the other prophecies pointing to Him whereas there are no references that in any way lead you directly to Muhammad. And in John 12:49–50 Jesus quotes Deuteronomy, verbatim, when He states that He speaks on God's behalf and not of His own initiative, 'therefore, the things I speak, I speak just as the Father has told Me.' There is just too much material that favors Jesus and nothing to support the idea that it was Muhammad those scriptures referred to.

"Another 'Red Herring' by Muslims is how proud they are to point out as a prophecy that Allah, Himself, promised to protect the Koran and keep it safe from any corruption (Surah 15:9). Once again they have a big problem. I have already told you how there were four or five versions (possibly as many as 27) of the Koran at one time. The one that survived was the most popular one, favored by those who were in power at the time while competing versions were destroyed. Their answer to that will be, 'See He protected the correct one.' But any objective person would have trouble with that explanation."

Herman couldn't help but smirk just a little, "One of the more silly claims to prophecy is their use of Sura 41:21 'Their skins will bear witness against them as to what they have been doing' to prove that the Koran prophesied the forensic technique of finger printing to catch criminals. But that idea ignores a whole range of other possible explanations, such as social diseases, getting sun burned from playing naked in the sun or even breaking out in hives from too much orange juice. Their explanation simply does not come close to being specific enough to convince anyone except a Muslim."

Herman then highlighted an amazing statistic. "Leroy, there are over three hundred prophesies in the Old Testament that are clearly fulfilled in the New Testament. For instance, the Prophet Mica predicts Jesus will be born in Bethlehem ... seven hundred years before it happens. Isaiah talks about the virgin birth, Zechariah describes the King riding on the foal of a donkey, Judas Iscariot's treachery is described in detail by David in Psalms, even his remorse when he threw the coins into the Synagogue is confirmed. That 'blood' money was used to buy the 'potter's field' (Matthew 27:7). We don't have time to go over every one of them but it is an overwhelming case for the accuracy of all those prophesies."

Out of nowhere, Herman jolted me with an obtuse question. "Leroy, what was the most painful physical event in your life?" Like a hunting dog on point I snapped to attention as I met his questioning gaze. It felt like I was back in the Marine Corps and a general was about to inspect my uniform and weapon.

"What," was all I could say for a moment? "What do you mean?"

"Leroy, if you want to get a real personal and intimate feeling for the prophecy of Christ's crucifixion you need to read Psalm 22:16–18 and at the same time think about the most painful physical event in your life. What was yours?"

My life began to pass before my eyes. At two years of age I had nearly chopped off half of my left foot with a large, two-edged, lumberjack style of an ax. But I had no memory of the event, let alone how it felt. Then there was the time when I was fourteen years old; I tried to take a butcher knife away from my younger brother, Raymon. I still remember the shooting pain as he suddenly jerked his hand free of my grasp and the blade of the knife sliced my right index finger to the bone. I still have the scar but the pain only lasted a few minutes. No, that one didn't qualify. A number of my most difficult races came to mind as I remembered how I desperately strained for the finish line with every muscle in my body freezing up, figuratively in rigor mortis.

No, that wasn't good enough. The joy of the race far outweighed the temporary clamping down of lactic acid.

This was a difficult question to answer on the fly. Even though I was not yet a Christian, I did believe in the crucifixion. Intellectually, I knew that His pain and suffering on the cross was light years out of my frame of reference for even beginning to understand the magnitude of that event. Unlike a finger being burnt by a flame, there was no way to pull back to escape. That was key. There was no way to diminish the pain, to escape the insult to the flesh, no place to go to lick your wounds and begin to recover.

Then I remembered an incident in Hillcrest Park (Fullerton) when I was about five years old. I was playing on a glider-swing. I was barefoot and stood up on the arm and began to rock the swing. But I was too close to the hinge. My right foot slipped and was crushed when it became trapped between the glider arm and the leg of the supporting A frame. I screamed but couldn't pull my foot out of the space between the arm and the frame. It seemed like an eternity before my Dad came running and moved the swing enough to pull my foot free. The pain left me crumpled and unable to do anything for myself for days. I had to wear special Health Spot boots for about three years to rebuild the arch.

Following Herman's prompting, I read Psalm 22:16–18, as I recalled the foot incident. "For dogs have surrounded me; a band of evildoers has encompassed me; they pierced my hands and my feet; I can count all my bones; they look, they stare at me;" and then came the clincher, "They divide my garments among them, and for my clothing they cast lots." Matthew 15:24 is virtually a direct quote of that Old Testament verse. Seemingly helpless and hopeless, it was prophesied that He would hang on that cross, unable to pull away; unable to escape the pain, and for what, or better still, who? It was irrefutable that this was an accurate and fulfilled prophecy. David wrote his Psalms more than 900 years before the crucifixion, long before anyone had even heard of the Romans and their habit of nailing people to a cross. What did Islam have to offer as an alternative? Muhammad died when he was about sixty-three years old of an illness or possibly from being poisoned, not as a sacrifice for anyone else. I could only conclude that Islam was a sham, a pretender at best.

We were both very quiet. I dabbed at my eyes trying not to cry. This felt very real and personal. There was no way I could pay for what was being offered. Between Christianity and Islam there was a great chasm. Islam could not compete. In my mind I was convinced but my heart, craving self-indulgence was not yet ready to follow.

Construct #3

INERRANCY

"Every word of God is tested; He is a shield to those who take refuge in Him. Do not add to His words lest He reprove you, and you be proved a liar." (Prov. 30:5–6)

"Errors in the Bible are a forgone conclusion to Muslims," said Herman, as he began his next explanation. "The first example they usually point to will be the multiple variations of the Bible as proof. They will argue that the King James Version, the New King James Version, the American Standard, the New American Standard, the New International Version, and the Revised Standard Edition are all corrupted by virtue of their use of different words and phrases. It is inconsistent but they pretty much accept the Old Testament because Islam claims most of the same prophets; the Old Testament doesn't call Jesus by name; it doesn't specifically talk about the Trinity; and the Israelites fought many battles against polytheists.

"But words such as 'New' and 'Version' in translation titles are dead giveaways to different interpretations of the New Testament, in their minds. This is a weak argument that oversimplifies historical facts and the messages taught through those facts. For example, we can look at Paul's ministry to illustrate that strict, word for word translations are not the goal and definitely not necessary. Getting the message to the listener in a way he/she can understand and relate to it is the objective. When Paul was converted on the road to Damascus, his name was Saul at the time. He soon became known as Paul because that was the name variation that Greeks and Romans were familiar with. This simple maneuver strengthened his ministry because his audiences could more easily identify with him and it really didn't change his identity in any material way. In addition, when he preached to the Gentiles, he tried to meet his audience where they were by speaking in a language (Paul spoke at least three and possibly four different languages) and style they could relate to. Using idioms and phrases they were familiar with broke down barriers of resistance without watering down the essentials of the Gospel he was proclaiming."

Seeking clarification, I asked, "So what you are saying is that different translations are somewhat like one person ordering a rainbow sherbet ice cream cone while another person orders an ice cream cone with orange, lime and raspberry flavored sherbet, right?"

Herman couldn't help but laugh out loud, "Leroy, I can always count on you to come up with awesomely simple explanations straight from the Ozarks. Yes, that pretty much says what I was meaning. If there were any Hillbilly Gentiles in Paul's audiences, they would have immediately understood the message."

I wasn't quite finished, "Couldn't we use the same argument you used for the Bible about what you say are contradictions in the Koran? Isn't there a case that those apparent contradictions are really just pedantic differences in stylistic and idiomatic usage? I mean, the use of the term a 'hanging thing' sounds a lot like an embryo attached to the uterine wall, to me."

Herman wasn't fazed in the least. "So, what you are asking is that if anything in that entire context makes sense, then we have to accept all of it as factual?"

That was enough for me. "Let's just move on."

"Maybe this will help. One of the most famous examples of Paul's ability to target a given audience is found in Acts. Paul had been preaching to already, God-fearing Jews in the synagogues of Athens but he wanted to branch out to a wider audience. Now remember, Paul was not your average camel jockey. He had received an outstanding education as the protégé of Gamaliel a very famous teacher. By today's standards, he probably had two or three PhDs. and a lot of post-doc. experience as well. As such, he had been taught and knew just about everything concerning Roman, Egyptian, Jewish and especially Greek societies and their histories. He was very much aware of the Greeks' love for discussing and arguing about anything new, so when they asked him to tell them about this 'new religion' he was more than ready. In fact, I doubt anyone but Paul would have recognized the opportunity this gave him. He went with them to the Aeropagus (Mars Hill, a public forum) and played them at their own game. He began with, 'I observe that you are very religious in all respects. For while I was passing through and examining the objects of your worship, I also found an altar with this inscription, TO AN UNKNOWN GOD' (Acts 17:23). You see he knew that the Greeks tried to cover all their bases. They were polytheistic and just in case they had accidently missed an important deity they put up a monument to the 'unknown god.' That was Paul's opening. He then announces that he has come to tell them about that unknown god. He had his audience in the palm of his hand. The Greeks got a full dose of pristine and accurate Gospel ... in their own language, in their own city and in their own intellectual style.

"On the other hand, Muslim's will be emphatic, almost to the point of rage that the Koran is perfect, that it has never been changed; that it is pure and has never been corrupted, like they claim the Bible has been. But Islam is an authoritative religion and their authorities have simply pounded them repeatedly on this point. Muslims believe it because their leaders have said it, ad infinitum. Say something often enough and a lot of people begin to believe it. The truth is when the Koran was finally written down, there were several versions. One by Zaid had 114 Surah, another by Ibin Mas'ud featured only 112 but another by Ubay had 116. Some were preferred by the Sunni and others by the Shia and the other various sects of Islam. The controversy over which one was the correct one was finally settled by simply publishing the one preferred by those in power and burning the others.[9] And, there are a number of errors in spelling, dates of particular events and the locations of those events. But the average Muslim would never know this because they are not even aware of the history of the Koran."

He then pointed out, "A lot of Muslims jumped on the bandwagon of a book that purports to prove a lot of errors in the Bible, especially in the New Testament. In doing so, they are in direct conflict with the Koran itself. As I have pointed out before, the Koran directs them to study the Injeel as the 'unchangeable' word of God.[10] Muhammad himself is emphatic that the Book (Torah, Psalms and the New Testament) was not only God inspired but that it was incorruptible. That is, the Bible as we know it today, which was already in existence in his lifetime was set in stone. It (Bible) was God's revealed word according to none other than Muhammad, himself. That doesn't faze modern Muslims. They simply ignore anything that doesn't fit their scornful idea about Christians and the Bible.

"The book, *Misquoting Jesus* by Bart D. Ehrman at first read is quite disturbing and makes a case that early scribes, who were virtually illiterate themselves either made errors when copying early, original Christian documents, or made changes because they thought they were correcting previous errors, or simply reworded some tests to convey what they thought was better. He correctly comes to the conclusion that many of the original, 'inspired' manuscripts have been lost but he is wrong to claim only erratic substitutes were all that was left to be later canonized into the Bible we have today. There are over 25,000 supporting manuscripts and other documents that confirm today's Bible is accurate."

Herman furrowed his brows, "The first problem I have with his book is the title. Misquoting Jesus is the basis of his theories but 90 to 95% of his book does nothing with things Jesus said. Now I have no problem that there are some copying errors over the centuries. But the crux of the problem is what do we mean by inerrant and 'Inspired Word' of God? Does that mean every word must be inspired or was the message inspired?" I was starting to get queasy. This conversation was headed into an erudite cosmos, very much to my personal displeasure.

He took no notice of my reluctance to engage. "Leroy, if I told you that Jesus Christ said you should eat chicken soup more often, what message would you take that to mean?" "Chicken soup? Aw come on H. What are you talking about?"

"Well, if next Sunday I preached a sermon on how Christ Jesus, himself, advocated eating more chicken soup, would you question who I was quoting?"

"Now you are getting downright silly," I complained.

"I suppose so." He went on anyway, "All the same, would you be confused whether I quoted Jesus, Christ, Christ Jesus or Jesus the Christ?"

Now I saw his point. "Of course not, they all are the same person."

He was beaming, "That's right and that is exactly one of my biggest problems with people like Ehrman. They demand literal preciseness dealing with the Bible. That threshold isn't found in any other historical records they believe in and rely on. He and others just like him will confidently quote Homer, Josephus, Ananus, Tacitus or Suetonius or any number of other historical figures, with a tenth of the corroborating support the Bible has.

"Hold on Herman. Who the heck are you talking about?" I pleaded.

"Well, they are all a bunch of recognized, legitimate historians that were anything but Christians themselves. And they wrote about Jesus, the Caesars, and just about everything in the first through the fourth centuries. They all give solid evidence to the accuracy and authenticity of the Bible, the same one we have today. The main point is the message in today's Bible is the 'Inspired Word' of God, no matter which translation is used."

He continued his attack on all detractors, "One of the biggest arguments presented by these kinds of antagonists, in an effort to discredit the Bible, especially the New Testament, is to complain that evidence presented by Christians is distorted by their reliance on 'within the Bible' sources. But they totally ignore that there are huge amounts of documents from more or less hostile historians like the ones I just told you about.

"He also plays pretty loose with numbers." He was starting to bark just a little. "For instance, lets say that a scribe accidentally wrote 'Jesus the Christ' rather than 'Christ Jesus.' And let's say that 'error' is copied thousands of times. He then states astronomical lists of errors in the thousands and thousands when in fact it was one error, transcribed multiple times." Herman saw that he was beginning to 'lose' me. "I'm sorry. I get a little worked up with these kinds of hacks. The point for you is that people like Ehrman will bowl you over in a one-on-one meeting. It takes a lot of scholarly research to counter people like that and most of us just don't have the horsepower to meet them head on. Just know that the work has been done and all the arguments in his book have been refuted by qualified people. Josh McDowell's book, *The New Evidence That Demands a Verdict* is the most complete, scholarly and convincing treatment of those facts and arguments that you will find on the shelf at Barnes and Noble."

Construct #4

UNDERSTANDABILITY

"Then He opened their minds to understand the scriptures,..." (Luke24:45)

Long before becoming a Christian, I believed any religion that required a PhD. to understand it, couldn't be much of a religion, especially for the common man. This was an area where Herman and I were 'simpatico.' Understandability was a crucially important construct for me. Without understanding, what good would it be, even if it were the most brilliant revelation of all time? If I were to engage Albert Einstein in a discussion about relativity, the result would be about as useful as 'teats on a boar' as my father would have said. To me, understandability equaled usefulness and thus believability. It was reassuring to me that Herman emphasized this construct, to the degree he did.

"The Bible is a literary marvel. An average person could pick it up and begin reading at any random book, and immediately understand the basics of the story. There would be a beginning, middle and an end. The protagonist and antagonist would be quickly recognized. Whether written in prose or poetry, as correspondence or love letters, the reader would very soon recognize a theme that dynamically progresses from a problem to a solution. Upon further study the reader would soon recognize sub-plots and trends. And a student of the entire Bible would begin to spot prophecies given and fulfilled; lines of heritage that would lead to a Messiah; promises made by God and then produced; and a message of hope and salvation that was personal and attainable." Herman was in pig heaven as he devoured his own explanations.

He was never satisfied with just explaining important things to you. He always supplied spot on and bold examples. "Leroy, have you ever heard of a guy named Watkin Roberts," he queried?

"Who," came my puzzled reply?

"This will take a little explaining," he said, "but it is a mind-blowing case study about how powerful the scriptures are, all alone, without commentaries or Cliff Notes." He was on the edge of his seat. "In 1910, a Welsh missionary by the name of Watkin Roberts went into a remote area of North East India, to evangelize the Hmar tribesmen who were notorious headhunters. He didn't have enough money to translate and publish the entire Bible. All he could afford to give them at the time was the Gospel of John. Plus, he was only able to stay with them for five days. In that short period, armed only with the book of John, five of the headhunters were convinced to 'give their names' to Jesus and they became pastors, themselves. It was later reported by various Missionaries that the Hmar tribe (60,000–80,000 estimated population) was 100% Christian, and the neighboring Mizo tribe (400,000 estimated population) also became 100% Christian, all in about 30–40 years[11]. How's that for understandability of the Bible?"

He then began to dissect the Koran. "Whereas the Bible flows from beginning to end with a recognizable story, the Koran, as a whole cannot be understood on it's own. It is divided into 114 chapters, called Sura, organized by length. The first Sura is fairly short but beginning with the second Sura (277 verses with about 12,000 words) they follow more or less in descending order down to the last one (5 verses with 36 words). Even the Imams cannot make sense of it by itself. To understand the Koran, you absolutely have to study the Sira and the Hadith because that is where Muhammad's life provides the examples of how to interpret the Koran," Herman emphasized.

"There is no timeline either. The Sura are totally random subject wise and chronologically. It is generally accepted that the average Muslim cannot understand the Koran without the help of someone who has spent years of study to unlock its messages and meanings through the light of accepted Sira and Hadith. Adding to the confusion there are many Sirah and Hadith that are considered less than reliable (approximately 4–6 versions are accepted as authentic, for each)."

Herman pointed out, "If you know the Bible well, the Koran becomes much more readable and informative. With knowledge of the Bible, you can fill in the timeline gaps and begin to see themes between the individual directives. But without that prior knowledge, I don't see how anyone could argue for understandability of the Koran," he concluded.

"From what you have just told me, I can't see it either," I had to agree.

Coup de Gras

"I am amazed that you are so quickly deserting Him who called you by the grace of Christ, for a different gospel: which is really not another; only there are some who are disturbing you and want to distort the gospel of Christ." (Galatians 1:6–7)

Herman began his summation with one more arrow to the heart of Koranic "gravitas." "You know, the truth is in spite of all the political correctness out there and all the excuses that you will hear defending the Koran and all the false arguments about equivalence, there is a simple and logical explanation to knock down those arguments. It deals with one very fundamental reality. The Koran is not original material!

"The proof of this can be found in how Muslim's are so very proud of the Koran and insist on its superiority over the Bible. They believe that no other book or writing can come close to the perfection of the poetry and wisdom found in it. One of their challenges is to dare you to show them any other book that comes close to the Koran's uniqueness. I accept that challenge and can prove otherwise rather quickly. All you have to do is hold the Bible in your left hand and an English version of the Koran in the right hand and begin reading back and forth from certain verses in the Bible then the Koran or vice versa. It is uncanny how the Koran not only supports the Bible, it actually begins to sound like direct quotes, as if it were a Reader's Digest version. It's almost like Muhammad is reading the Bible then has an epiphany to add his own understanding to it. The Koran doesn't tell the whole story but it highlights things Muhammad wanted to emphasize." Herman reprised his earlier point, "Indeed, the Koran makes a lot more sense if you know the Bible first. Unfortunately, it is not in chronological order so this exercise can be very difficult.

"Let's go back to the apartment so I can grab my Koran and we can play a game to illustrate how closely the Koran follows the Bible."

Five minutes later, back at the apartment, Herman reached for his Koran on the bookshelf. "There are 114 Sura, (chapters) pick a number between 1 and 114"

"OK," I replied, "I'm in. My number is XXVIII because I'm 28 years old."

"Great. Now pick a verse number."

"Well, I don't want to break my pattern so my verse number is 28 again."

"Terrific. Now here's how we play the game. I'm going to open the Koran to Sura XXVIII, verse 28 and I predict that within five verses just prior or just after, I will find something that sounds very familiar, virtually right from the Bible itself. Ok, here we go. **Bingo!** Leroy, you really are amazing. In verse 29 we read, 'And when Moses had fulfilled the term (working for his father-in-law) and was journeying with his family, he perceived a fire on the mountain side.' Then in verse 30, 'And when he came up to it, a voice cried to him out of the bush from the right side of the valley in the sacred hollow. O Moses, I truly am God, the Lord of the Worlds.' Herman was grinning from ear to ear. "Does that sound familiar to you?"

"Well if that don't beat a hen a peck..."

"Stop it! Please spare me," cried Herman!

"Let me see that," I demanded as I grabbed the Koran and reread verse 29. "Wow! That is incredible. Let's try LXXXII, my age backwards and verse 82," I suggested as I handed it back.

"OK, let's try it," he quickly agreed. "Woops! Can't do it. There are only 12 verses in that Sura, but that's fine. Let's start in the middle at verse six and go up 5 or down 5 verses and see what we find." Herman remained confident. "Well, well, what do you know about that? Look at verse 10. 'Yet truly there are guardians over you—Cognizant of your actions. Surely amid delights shall the righteous dwell, but verily the impure in Hell-fire.' What does that sound like to you?"

I was not up to speed for finding stuff in the Bible, but "man alive" that sounded a lot like the Book of Life and Judgment Day to me.

"Now this does not work with every Sura because some of the verses are simply greetings or closing statements and some of them are so short (3–4 verses) that nothing significant is stated and there are a few original statements as well." Herman then summed up his point. "Muhammad would get an F in a creative writing class because the Koran looks more like a 'knock off' of the Bible than a brilliant original. The Koran isn't unique or superior at all. It is 114 chapters of plagiarism but without the complete stories! And you can repeat this game with many (but not all) other Sura with pretty much the same results," he happily surmised (see Appendix B). "How in the world can the Koran be superior to the Bible? In reality it is only a commentary on the Bible not a competing book!"

He usually avoided "overkill" in these kinds of discussions but today he was more 'into' it and kept plugging along. "Another instance that seems to point to the Bible as the precedent and all encompassing document is Sura 10:38 where it says, 'Moreover this Koran could not have been devised by any but God: but it confirmith what was revealed before it and is a clearing up of the Scriptures (Bible)-there is no doubt thereof-from the Lord of all creatures.' In other words, we needed Muhammad to further explain Biblical scriptures because the current Jews and Christians were missing God's true intent. You see, the Bible as we know it today had already been in existence for about 250 years and somehow, even though he was illiterate, Muhammad was very familiar with it. But all around him he witnessed idolatry and polytheism. And when Christians proclaimed the Trinity, to him they were adding two more gods to God. This was blasphemous polytheism. And so, even though the Bible strictly forbids adding or subtracting to the scriptures (Proverbs 30:5, Revelation 22:18–19), he sincerely believed he was a prophet, chosen by God to expose this error. The Koran is really not much more than Muhammad's enlargement or clarification of the Bible."

I was already impressed and pretty much convinced but he had just a little more. "I have barely scratched the surface with the four constructs. What I've told you today isn't much more than an introduction to a full academic review. If we wanted to study this comparison of the two books in depth, we would have to also look at constructs in reliability, historicity, internal and external evidence, scientific evidence, and counter arguments from both sides. I can tell you there are libraries full of this sort of material and it all supports the Bible over the Koran, hands down." Now he was finished.

Chapter 4

TRANSFORMATION

How in The World Did I Get Here?

"And do not be conformed to this world, but be transformed by the renewing of your mind, that you may prove what the will of God is, that which is good and acceptable and perfect." (Romans 12:2)

Saturday, August 25, 1973, 1:30 PM, Trinity Lutheran Church, San Gabriel, California: Sitting in the Grooms room Herman and I are waiting for the signal to enter the Sanctuary and stand in front of three hundred and fifty guests. I am fidgety and nervous but incredibly happy. How in the world did I ever get to this place in only two years? At thirty-two years of age I am elated that at last I have found a "knockdown" gorgeous someone who has said "yes" and apparently she really meant it. It was still a mystery to me that she endured my idiosyncrasies, flashes of anger and rude behaviors let alone wanted to grow old with me. I had become a Christian only a few months earlier and I still had some rough edges when compared to her Master of Arts Degree in Theology, from Fuller Theological Seminary right there in Pasadena.

About 15 minutes before we are due to "pull the trigger" Herman asks me, "Leroy, are you sure about this? If you have any doubts, I would rather have you embarrassed than to enter into such a commitment and it only lasts a few years or less. If you have any reservations, we can just slip out the back door and go get a beer."

He meant well but Pastor Mees had just entered the room in time to hear everything. "What in the world are you doing?" he gasped, as he turned pale with disbelief.

"I know and I am sure," I replied, to Pastor Mees's great relief (see Appendix A, 7).

It was not an outrageous question. In the two years we had roomed together and the next two years while I worked for Los Angeles County, he had watched my metamorphosis. We had known each other since 1955 and he was well aware of my history in relationships. His question was meant for the protection of me from myself and my bride's protection as well. He had experience in this area and knew of what he spoke.

Two years is not very long for the number and scope of the changes that had taken place in my life in that short span. I had finally studied the scriptures Herman had given me back at Buddy's. I did not understand them fully at first and I certainly resisted some of their messages. But the hole in my life that Herman had referred to needed to be filled with something substantial and lasting. It was an "on again, off again, Finnegan" personal wrestling match for those two years after Herman moved out of my apartment in San Diego. It had been an incredibly dramatic turn of events yet the day of transformation itself had come and gone almost unnoticed by anyone. More changes in my worldview and especially my newfound life in Christ, occurred in that span, than in the thirty-one previous years. I was different from the inside out.

The crisis over, Herman went to check on the rest of the Groom's Men and Pastor Mees returned to his office to retrieve his notes. Alone for a few minutes I began to review the events that lead up to this day. When Herman had predicted my grades would improve, I am quite sure he didn't have any idea of the eventual magnitude of that change. Sure enough, my grades climbed to the heady heights of C+ territory at FJC and Oxy. Grad.

school was another story, altogether. My first goal at San Diego State was to make up an academic minor in History to complete the Fisher Bill requirements for teaching in the California public schools. I assumed I would become a high school track coach, by default. I simply had no real plans. I decided to get that requirement out of the way in one large dose. For the spring semester of 1969 I registered to take four history classes: Ancient Rome, Modern France, American Foreign Policy and Political History of 19th Century Europe. Each class required 5–6 lengthy papers and between 6 and 10 books to be read and all exams would be by "Blue Book." I was going to find out if I could make it in this one semester or quit wasting time in school. However, I had three very big problems. I had never written a paper before; I had taken only a couple of Blue Book exams before; and I had never read a serious book in my entire life.

But something odd happened as I ploughed into the task. First, not a soul on campus knew or cared if I went to class, let alone studied the material. Coach Bush was nowhere to be found. He was not checking up on me. Everything was entirely up to me. Then, as radical as it may sound, I found the library. The biggest surprise of all was when I opened my books and began to read ... I LIKED IT! I hungered for it! Then I began to write papers ... I LIKED THAT TOO! Who could have guessed? Even the Blue

Book exams were eagerly looked forward to ... because I knew the answers. It was heady stuff.

Going into the final weeks of the semester I was carrying four A's. And it didn't hurt my feelings at all that a number of very cute co-eds were asking for my advice or if I would help them study. I wasn't able to keep it up however. When reality caught up with me, I finished the semester with four Bs. But even four Bs was a monstrous academic transformation! I got one more B, and the then all A's, for the rest of Grad. School. I then produced a credible Master's Thesis, "A Comparison of Rate and Load Bicycle Ergometer Variables in The Assessment of Maximal Oxygen Uptake." It was published and filed in the school library.

Reading pertinent articles in medical and physiology journals and making note cards from those sources became an obsession to the point believe it or not, my social life was often postponed or just plain neglected. I enjoyed the research and writing necessary for the thesis so much that I thought at the time, "maybe some day I will write a book."

Rooming with Herman those two years was good for both of us. As you would expect, we continued to have many discussions on "love, life and the Republic." I now thought of myself as quite the intellectual and relished crossing swords with Herman on rational versus spiritual arguments about Christianity, Eastern

Mysticism and of course our old friend, Islam. I prospered in the classroom and he put his life back together. He didn't go back into his law practice but changed direction to become incredibly successful in IT areas such as encryption and computer programming. So much so, that he soon became quite famous and in constant demand for his unique and insightful approach to solving technical problems.

Everything went so well he also remarried. I was Best Man for him and Gloria Mendoza a beautiful Latina. Her father had brought me up to speed on all the traditions for a Mexican wedding and I gave the toasts at the right times and led out in the "Dollar Dance" to help finance their honeymoon. And now he was about to return the favor as my Best Man.

After getting my Masters Degree at San Diego State, I had gone to work for the Los Angeles County, Occupational Health Services as an Exercise Physiologist. My duties included conducting the Physical Fitness tests for LA County Deputy Sherriff and Fire Department applicants. My lab was in room B-50 in the basement of the Hall of Administration, located in downtown Los Angeles.

I met and became friends with a young nurse who worked in the same department. Shannon was a Christian and lived in Pasadena with three other Christian girls. We began to talk quite a lot about what it meant to be a Christian and she took me to church with her a few times at a small building up in Altadena just north of downtown Pasadena. My position at the time was that all religions were pretty much alike and I was somewhat interested in Eastern Mysticism that I had been reading about.

Eventually she convinced me to attend a Navigator's Conference in Idyllwild, California, a mountain retreat near Palm Springs. Between her urging and Herman's scriptures I was at a tipping point with only one remaining obstruction. Graduate school had puffed me up into an intellectual snob with disdain for anything I could not touch, taste, smell, hear or see. My acceptance of anything depended upon its measurability. I was a scientist! This was the last hurdle blocking my acceptance of Jesus as Lord and Savior. Everything else had begun to make sense. Morality, honesty, respect for others and the "Golden Rule" no longer put me off or threatened my freedom. I felt very good about those kinds of changes in my life. What I didn't know was that Shannon and her roommates had been praying for me for several months. Apparently, Herman wasn't the only one who believed in the efficacy of that practice.

In the Spring of 1973 I went to the retreat. It was providential! The keynote speaker was Dr. Duane Gish of the Creationist Institute in San Diego. The topic was a review and deeper explanation of his most recent publication, *EVOLUTION: the fossils say, NO*. He laid out a sound presentation of facts that finally removed my last straw dog. Science and Christianity were no longer incompatible. When he finished and made the "Altar Call" I popped up and lurched forward. I was still resisting but someone had placed their hand in the middle of my back and continued pushing me forward, even though I leaned back and attempted to block my own forward progress by bracing my feet against the floor. It didn't work. It was an intense 'approach, avoidance' behavior moment. I was forced onward, virtually "kicking and screaming" as I advanced toward heaven. When I arrived at the altar I looked around to see who had pushed me. **There was no one there!** I knelt down and confessed my sins. Returning to my seat I felt as light as a feather. Something very big had happened. It felt huge but when I returned home no one was aware of it or noticed a difference in my behavior or attitude except Shannon and her roommates.

In the mean time Herman was doing cartwheels and back flips as I kept him up to speed on my job and my newfound interest in studying the scriptures he had given me. When I described my conversion experience to him and the non-reaction of my family and friends he reminded me of a few things.

"Leroy, I hope you didn't go into this thing expecting everyone to scrape and bow as if you were some kind of hero. Do not compare yourself to St. Paul or Raul Ries or Chuck Colson or anyone else. When they were converted it was a very big and public deal because of where they came from. You on the other hand, whether you realize it or not, were not very far away at all. I have a theory I call the 'Christian Conversion Continuum.' It is really quite simple. The farther a person is away from God at the time of their conversion, the more dramatic and public it will usually be (but not always) externally, and more than likely that person will soon have a mission in the same area they just come from. St. Paul went from rounding up Christians for execution to become a martyr himself. Raul Ries went from gangbanger to evangelizing gangs. Chuck Colson went from prisoner to ministering to prisoners. Your transformation was not all that dramatic externally and it will probably take a while for you to recognize your own ministry but it is a certainty that you will have one."

He then contrasted my conversion to a comparison between St. Augustine and C.S. Lewis. St. Augustine had gone through a long, protracted and excruciatingly physical as well as spiritual struggle, leading up to transformation. Much less dramatic, C. S. Lewis took a bus ride to the zoo. When he got on, he was an atheist. When he got off, he was a "Born Again" full fledged, totally committed Believer and soon became a world famous Christian apologist. "Whether one is driven almost to madness in the moment of the new birth, or experiences it quietly on a bus to the zoo, the reality is in fact stupendous. Nothing is more important for two human souls than to say truly, 'We know that we have passed out of death into life (1John 3:14).'[1]

"Leroy, the most important thing for you to realize is how close and personal your conversion was. It was very intimate. Jesus was meeting you at exactly the place you needed Him the most. Be grateful that you did not need a physical spanking. Above all, you should know that every conversion is dramatic and life changing, internally. You are no longer the person you were for thirty-two years. You are a new creation. And you shouldn't be disappointed if people are not in awe of your personal story even though you have every bit as much spiritual power as anyone who has ever lived or will be born in the future. Just keep plugging away until you know what you mission field is and then embrace it. Somewhat like that Jesus-Person back at San Diego State, your job is to love God with your whole heart, not to find meaning in what others think or say about you!" Herman beseeched me.

"One of the reasons I remained your friend all these years was I could see how much you wanted a Christian life in spite of your life style. All those years of your grandmother's flannel board stories, your family going to church when you were young, your older brother taking you to church even when your parents didn't go, your athletic experiences under Coach Bush, your experiences in Viet Nam, the four girls praying for you, all together built a value system within you that kept edging you inch by inch closer to this very day. You didn't know it, but from the outside you began to look every bit like a Christian.

"Of course, you did live a pretty loose and free life-style for years. Your friends and family got used to that persona. You shouldn't be too hard on them for not recognizing how much you have changed. You earned that reputation! But I can guarantee you that they are thrilled about it. And don't expect them to immediately forget what for thirty-two years you trained them to see in you. It is going to take quite some time for them to trust that the new you is for real."

"When you are right, you are right," I finally admitted.

Herman continued to cross-examine me on everything, especially my friend Shannon. I dated her a few times but our relationship was not progressing. We were more than just friends but there was no serious direction either. One day we stopped by for a cup of tea in the kitchen of a beautiful, old, two-story Victorian house where she lived with her roommates, a mere "stones throw" from the Rose Bowl. That's when **IT** happened!

Gail Moe, one of the roommates came home from her own date and passed through the kitchen where Shannon introduced us. Blonde and blue-eyed, she was a dazzling beam of sunlight and I felt an electric charge run through my entire body. She was polite but showed no real interest in me. She said she was glad to meet me and went to her room. She had absolutely no idea what was coming her way. The next day I called Herman and told him, "I have met the girl I am going to marry!"

"Well it's about time," he chided with relief. When I told him who it was, there was silence at his end of the phone for about thirty or forty seconds. He finally pulled himself together. "How in the world are you going to pull it off?" he demanded, incredulously.

All I could say at the time was, "I don't know but God will provide."

Eventually I managed to catch Gail home alone on a Saturday afternoon at that old Victorian house. On a whim, we went up to B & H Ranch, a bar about two miles straight up Fair Oaks Ave. in Altadena. We ordered a beer then I leaned across the table and kissed her. It was the most sensual kiss I had ever experienced. It is said that lightning never strikes the same place twice, but another very large electric charge ran through my body, right down to my socks. The next day, after she came home from church, we hiked up Mallard Canyon (in the foothills behind Altadena) to a beautiful waterfall. Nine days later we were engaged and as they say, the rest is history.

Forty-two years, two children and a thirty-five year track coaching career later Gail and I retired to Colorado Springs. The move was an age-old fait accompli. The tail that wags all retirees' dog, our two sons and the grandchildren had moved to Colorado Springs (see Appendix A-6). It was a fairly easy adjustment and we quickly settled in and soon found a church that fit us to a tee.

Grandchildren aside, new environments, new neighbors and new pastors can trigger a personal reformation. In my case, it was of gigantic proportions. So much so that one particular sermon at our new church home snowballed into a life changing experience.

Radical Conversions and Soft Landings

"'Saul, Saul, why are you persecuting Me?' And he (Saul) said, 'Who art thou, Lord?' 'I am Jesus whom you are persecuting.'" (Acts 9:4–5, NAS)

It's the first Sunday of Epiphany, January 4, 2015. I'm in my usual seat at Holy Cross Lutheran Church, Colorado Springs, Colorado. Center aisle, fifth row back, first seat on the right. I'm alone. Gail is sick and stayed home. After the preliminary liturgy, Pastor Dave Hall begins his sermon on the Riches of God. We are lucky here at Holy Cross to have three full-time pastors who take turns delivering great sermons. Today is no exception. At approximately 8:40 AM Pastor Hall cites Acts 9, the conversion of Saul on the road to Damascus to illustrate an important point, "and suddenly a light from heaven flashed around him; and he fell to the ground and heard a voice saying to him, "Saul, Saul, why are you persecuting Me?" Saul is blinded temporarily in this confrontation and asks, "Who are you Lord?" When Jesus Himself answered, I felt a chill and sat up ramrod straight. I must confess I didn't hear another word of the sermon. I totally missed any point this passage was supposed to illustrate.

Since my conversion in Idyllwild in 1973 I had attended hundreds of Bible studies and came to Acts 9 uncountable times. But I had always breezed right on through it. I would muse to myself, "Yes, yes, Saul is converted! Now let's get on to the good stuff . . . his magnificent ministry." My underestimation of the importance of this event is staggering, in retrospect. Arguably this was the beginning of the most radical conversion in the history of Christianity. Saul then became known as Paul and is responsible for half of the New Testament. And now Jesus is giving him the job of taking the Gospel to the Gentiles and really the rest of the entire world. Paul changes course from rounding up Christians for execution to eventually becoming a martyr himself. This was a big deal! More than radical, it was transformative of the early Church. Without Paul, Christianity might have remained a small, Jewish sect. His impact upon the early church cannot be overestimated. It was **RADICAL!**

Suddenly my mind's eye began to flash neon signs of **RADICAL! RADICAL! RADICAL!** My imagination ran amuck. Undisciplined it flashed to Ft. Hood where Captain Hassan, a Muslim radical shot and killed thirteen people;[2] then to Ottawa where another Muslim radical attacked the Parliament building;[3] and then to Oklahoma where yet another radical Muslim beheaded a woman.[4]

For some unknown reason, I began to think in "radical" pairs. What if I compared Paul to the Ottawa shooter? The Ottawa shooter came from an Islamic background to attack the legal system of Canada. Paul was a religious zealot who came with the power of the Jewish legal system to attack Christianity. Hmmmmm! This comparison was dramatic to say the least.

Next, I reached way out into left field and snatched C.S. Lewis to be paired with Captain Hassan. Lewis was a fellow at Magdalene College, Oxford, England and a gifted intellectual who addressed the ills and foibles of society with his writing.

Lewis began as a non-believer. In fact, he set out to disprove Christianity. In the process, he not only became a Christian but a famous apologist.

Captain Hassan was well educated also with degrees in Biology, Biochemistry, Osteopathy and Psychiatry. He used his intellectual abilities as a psychiatric counselor to address the ills and foibles of soldiers returning from war zones. And then he attacked the infidels! It would appear that Lewis and Hassan began with a few things in common but experienced completely opposite trajectories. This comparison was intensified by its juxtaposition. One used the "sword" and the other battled with his "pen" to achieve their objectives.

Once more I reached into my bag of the implausible, the ridiculous, the... well you get the idea. What if I paired Alton Nolen who beheaded his Christian co-worker, with Rochunga Pudaite? Who was Pudaite? He was the son of Chawnga, one of the original five headhunters who became pastors in Manipur, India. He came from that same tribe in remote NE India that Watkin Roberts had evangelized some ninety-five years earlier. At the age of ten he walked 96 miles out of the jungle, began his education, eventually graduated from Wheaton College, then earned an MA in Education at Northern Illinois University. He then received an honorary Doctorate of Divinity from Dallas

Baptist University. Not yet finished, he next, amongst many other things, founded Bibles for the World and translated the Bible into the Hmar language for his tribe in India.

It was an easy step to compare Pudaite and Nolen. Pudaite came from a tribe of headhunters to become a world famous Christian "heart hunter."[5] Nolen came from a fanatical, Islamic position to become a "head hunter." This paring begs for an explanation of each convert's driving motivation. However, with or without explanation it is apparent that a better understanding of the fundamentals of both Islam and Christianity is needed. Once more I was stunned at the ironies of these pairs.

"Herman, where in the world are you? I need you to help me process this. I don't understand and this is scary stuff," I whispered to myself. But Herman remained elusive. I had lost track of him just after our fortieth high school reunion in 1999. One day we had a heated debate of whether our involvement in the Kosovo War was part of Bill Clinton's attempt to deflect attention away from his impeachment trial or whether Jesse Ventura's election as governor was a serious attempt to solve economic problems in Minnesota; then nothing for the next sixteen years. It was as if he had dropped off the face of the earth. No phone call, no letter, absolutely nothing as to what had happened to him. I had tried to contact his father but he had disappeared also.

His mother had passed away from cancer, five years earlier. All other relatives were in Pakistan and I didn't dare contact them. Even the Alumni offices at FUHS, Princeton and Harvard were dead ends. The only clue I had about his disappearance was his alluding to some personal problems at our fortieth reunion and the possibility of traveling to Palestine for some research. It was very odd that he had referred to his destination as Palestine and I wondered, what possible research could only be done there and not from home?

I felt abandoned as I contemplated these wild and disturbing flashes of insight. They conjured up question after question about my own faith in comparison to Islam. It was a cold realization that I would be "in over my head" if I were to engage in a discussion comparing Islam to Christianity, with any devout Muslim, let alone an Imam. I had no idea of where to begin or how to defend my faith in such a confrontation. But it wasn't just Islam that had me confounded. The drama of Paul's conversion seemed to shine a light on my own conversion to the point I was confused about what we shared in common. To be sure, we shared a lot, conceptually. But spiritually and emotionally, did we have the same experience? My conversion was noticeably non-dramatic and went virtually unnoticed. I didn't sell everything I owned, let alone give it to the poor and I certainly didn't disappear into the jungles of central Africa to save some indigenous tribe. As a result, I have often referred to my conversion as a "soft landing." My life continued on pretty much as before ... peacefully. Herman had always been my sounding board for these kinds of situations. As I recalled our many discussions about Islam and conversion, I longed for his reassurance.

Obviously, I was on my own this time. I could only imagine the approach Herman would have taken. So I decided to tackle this situation as if he were here with me and I would try to argue and discuss it with myself from two perspectives, from the biased position of what it looked and felt like from the inside and then trying to look at myself from an objective, outside view.

So Just What Is the Problem?

"For God is not a God of confusion but of peace, as in all the churches of the Saints ... But all things must be done properly and in an orderly manner." (1 Corinthians 14:33, 40)

Pastor Hall's sermon was not to blame for my confusion. How could it be? I missed at least half it. It was my inability to process one very basic Biblical reference that led to my poignant moment. My frame of reference had been jarred. What this confused moment revealed was my lack of thorough study of that particular verse. My penchant for impatience had rewarded me with a lack of depth when studying Acts 9 in the past. It was a good thing that I finally recognized I had a problem with this verse. It was unsettling enough to get me up off the couch to rethink a few old things while researching to find out new stuff. Things I should have already known. Paul was talking directly to me when he said, "I gave you milk to drink, not solid food; for you were not ready to receive it. Indeed, even now you are not yet able" (1 Corinthians 3:2).

My problem was a case of superficial Bible study and a large dose of naiveté about Islam. I needed a plan to correct these two problems. Without a doubt, Herman's first move would have been to retrieve the proper "tools." So my first task would be searching the scriptures for application and prayer for guidance. That was not all that scary a task but comparing Islam to Christianity was above my pay grade. I had a great deal to reexamine and even more to learn. My solution? Write a book and research the dual problems until I could finally breathe again. You are now reading the results of that effort.

What's So Radical About That?

"So then, you will know them by their fruits. Not everyone who says to me, 'Lord, Lord,' will enter the kingdom of heaven, but he who does the will of My Father who is in heaven." (Matthew 7:20–21)

Looking back, I now appreciate even more, Herman's advice about my conversion and it's lack of "splash" or public display. But the comparison with Paul was niggling at my self-image or more accurately my sense of coming up a little short of some perceived, grand goal.

I remembered discussing it one time with my father when I asked him, "How do I know that I have the Holy Spirit in me? I don't feel any different and I am very stoic in church, showing very little emotion."

He laughed and immediately told me, "Son, you got it in you. I know because of the work I see you do with your athletes. You demonstrate it everyday in the way you love them and try to mentor them."

Gradually it began to dawn upon me that the missing link to explaining my conundrum was a clear understanding of the different motivations for conversion, radical or not. Especially puzzling was my inability to wrap my mind around what motivated someone to violence in the name of religion. It was counterintuitive. Isn't "peace" a core principle to all religions? Isn't that one of the anchors of their very existence? In Exercise Physiological terms we would call it the law of "homeostasis," the return to a biological state of rest or balance. Everything is working just right and humming along ... quietly ... without stress.

So, just what was my motivation? What was Paul's? And the 'sore thumb' sticking out, what motivated Capt. Hassan, Michael Zehaf-Bibeau in Ottawa and especially Alton Nolen? We all must have felt something very strong to change our lives so much, whether it was on public display or an internal explosion. Something moved us to do today, what was totally unthinkable only yesterday. What was the same and what was different in each case? As for C. S. Lewis, Paul and Rochunga Pudaite, their motivations are easily demonstrated by the lives they led and the great works they accomplished after conversion.

At this point I could only be somewhat presumptuous about the motivation of others. For myself it was more a case of trying to be honest and accepting of where I was and who I was. True, everyone can easily regard their own shortcomings as an explanation that moved them to make a change for the better. I was selfish, self-absorbed, egotistical, overly indulgent in sensual gratification from personal relationships, ad infinitum. But the 'need' itself was not to be found in simply changing my behavior in those areas. A change in behavior would be the result of filling the true 'need.' What was it? It finally hit me! It had been right there in front of me from my first semester in the Exercise Physiology laboratory. Homeostasis! There's that word again. Man was made in God's image, perfect, in balance (at rest) with God's purposes and in fellowship with Him. Ever since the "Big Miss" in the Garden of Eden, man has been out of balance with God but his very nature is constantly striving to regain that balance. The emptiness in my life could only be filled when I returned to my natural home, in balance with God. I needed to confess and be "reborn" into homeostasis with God.

This does not mean, by any stretch of the imagination, that we will ever regain what we had in the Garden of Eden. It is simply recognition of the problem and the need to be in community with God, every day, every minute. Once we return to God our behaviors will begin to reflect that relationship but they will never be perfect again, of and by themselves. We are perfect, only in the saving grace of Jesus Christ.

By comparison, what are we to make of Radical Islam converts? What was the unmet need that drove them to violence? Don't they have the same hole in their lives that Christian converts have? Logically we would have to say yes, to be consistent with our understanding of what happened in the Garden of Eden. If this is true, then why don't they recognize what we see as the answer to their unmet need? Where does the homeostatic urge get derailed? My thought is that, for whatever reason, some people are more easily persuaded to take what seems to be a short cut and/or are more vulnerable to an emotional response.

Take a look at "road rage." I remember the Walt Disney classic, Motor Mania staring Goofy as Mr. Walker and his alter ego Mr. Wheeler. It is an age-old case of wanting revenge when things happen to you that you can't control. When they finally have the power to "do something" many people give in to anger and will run you right off the road if you even think about cutting in front of them. Others accept that which they don't control and rely on God to see them through. Who, more the Job might have responded in anger? Daniel, Jeremiah and Joseph choose to honor God rather than the natural instinct for revenge. Moses struck a rock with his staff to get water for his people and God punished him for it because he did it out of anger.

Ever since I had thought I was going to enroll at UCLA I had been a huge fan of the athletic programs there. Who wouldn't recognize the greatness of coaches like Johnny Wooden and Ducky Drake, not to mention famous athletes such as C. K. Yang and

Rafer Johnson. But when I first came back from Viet Nam I was so rapped up in Grad. School that I paid little attention to sports. In the lab, however, where I did most of my research there were a couple of guys who were big Laker fans. They talked a lot about the Lakers nemesis with the Milwaukee Bucks, Kareem Abdul-Jabbar. Their talk reminded me of two of my favorite athletes, Lew Alcindor and Keith Wilkes. I wanted to know how they were doing. They looked at me like I had been in another Galaxy, not Viet Nam. When I found out that they had both become Muslims, I was totally confused. Then there was Cassius Clay who had become Muhammad Ali.

Around the same time, I read two books dealing with race relations, the hot topic of the 60s and early 70s. The first was the biography of Malcom X and then the classic, *Black Like Me* by John Howard Griffin. There was a pattern here of lots of anger and a sense of disenfranchisement. Sure, there were lots of civil rights issues but Alcindor, Clay and even Malcom X came from Christian families. What changed? In the case of Malcom X, I could easily understand the seething rage after as a child he watched white men tie his father up and lay him on some railroad tracks to be cut in half when a train ran over him. But in general, what was the unmet need? I recognized that "60–90% of all converts to Islam in the US are African-American ... and 80%

of those converts were raised in the Christian church."[6] How did Islam fill the unmet need better than Christianity? I didn't find a satisfying answer then and it goes somewhat unresolved still. But I have some guesses and at best they are only guesses.

So what's the analog of anger and disenfranchisement in the case of Islamic conversion? Islam is very simplistic and authoritarian. You don't have to make any decisions, just follow orders. It's a little like your father says, "Go punch that kid in the face because he gave you a dirty look." It gives you an excuse and a target. All you have to do is blow something up. "Yeah! That will show you how angry I am!" My guess is that anger is probably the single biggest reason for radical conversions to Islam in the US. And where do we find large numbers of angry people who feel they have been treated unfairly? Prisons maybe? *Son of Hamas* author Mosab Yousef expressed this aberration perfectly, "I had become a radical just because I wanted to destroy something."[7]

As a general observation, I would say that it is more common to be angry than to be forgiving. To forgive and attempt to reconcile is a lot of extremely hard work and even more important, it requires taking responsibility for your own condition. I believe that this is one of the defining differences between Islam and Christianity. Both turn their lives over to God (Allah) but

Christians accept responsibility for their actions while the Muslim cites Allah's orders to excuse their violent actions. Demonstrating anger is the easiest of all emotions. Little wonder there is so much of it on display, everywhere you look.

It would be short sighted and naïve to presume that anger is the only reason for conversion to radical Islam in the US. As in the Crusades there are those who 'join up' seeking excitement and adventure. And there are undoubtedly many young folks who simply want to rebel or perhaps out of conscience, sympathize with a group seemingly under attack. And Community organizers fall all over themselves to rescue the unfairly treated Muslims. But the flagship of this phenomenon is anger.

Applying this over simplification to the great athletes I have admired all these years would be unfair and unctuous. They have always demonstrated that they are very intelligent and principled people, to my knowledge. But this explanation does seem to fit the radicals noted earlier. And more to the point, to be a "moderate Muslim" requires something the Christian simply can't do. They have to ignore major segments of the very foundation of their own faith. Islam is little more than high-sounding platitudes in the Koran without the applications supplied by the examples of Muhammad's life, Islam's foundational base. That is where the fundamentalist finds justification for violence. Muhammad was a violent and vengeful warrior with a "scorched earth" approach to spilling the blood and plundering of anyone who was not Muslim. His life and actions established the "fundamentals" of Islam and that does speak directly to resolving my confusion about radical conversions, Muslim or Christian. The radical Christian is adamant and public about his/her faith. The radical Muslim demonstrates his/her fundamental faith with acts of violence. It is not a surprise that we sometimes hear, "The radical Christian builds hospitals and the radical Muslim fills them up."

I could only hope that Herman would be proud of me as to my efforts to understand and defuse the hand grenades going off all around me.

Chapter 5

FORTIETH REUNION

——— ❋ ———

Changes

*"Therefore if anyone is in Christ, he is a new crea-
ture; the old things have passed away; behold,
new things have come." (2 Corinthians 5:17)*

Saturday, October 2, 1999, 8:30 pm, Sequoia Club, Buena
Park, CA: Everyone and everything is different. Gone is the
pretense and any attempt to camouflage who we are and what we
are. By far, the most common topics of the conversations are now
about hip replacements, heart-bypass surgeries and grandchildren. I actually knew quite a few of the people attending and even
liked them. Most welcome was the general sense of camaraderie
and the openly friendly "howdy's" and "what have you been up

to's." Perhaps everyone becomes a little more philosophical and nostalgic with age.

Gail and I found a quiet table where we could wait for Herman and Gloria. The band was pretty good and we danced a couple of times and had a glass of White Zinfandel as we watched the other dancers on the ballroom floor. I had met Herman earlier that day for lunch. Buddy's had been torn down years ago and a Bank of America branch had taken its place. The Hillside Drive-in on Brea Blvd. and the Bean Hut in Anaheim had also disappeared long ago. In N Out Burger was the closest thing to our old hangout, so it was our choice, by default.

Herman looked very different when he sauntered in. He was sporting a pretty good imitation of a Ulysses S. Grant beard except that his was jet black and he was wearing a Nehru shirt. "Well look at what the cat drug in," I declared.

"Jealous?" he came back.

After the mandatory hugs and backslaps we put away a couple of "double-doubles" and began our checklist of personal activities before we got serious. "Herman, you look different. What's going on with the new look? Is that what you wear for those computer seminars, that you charge outrageous prices for?" I wondered.

"Well, actually I don't do that anymore. I've gone back into my law practice in DC and it is going pretty well. As far as the outfit goes, I just felt that I needed a change. I was too predictable. And there for a few months I was a little depressed about changing careers and a few personal problems didn't help. But now, everything is going great and I am pretty excited about my practice."

I was a little envious. "Wow! I'm happy with my coaching career but I certainly don't make the kind of money you do."

"Money isn't everything, right? How 'bout you and Gail? Any regrets?" he asked.   "It's funny you ask that. Just a couple of days ago we were talking about that very thing. We were both amazed at what we have been through, how much we both had to change and the odds against it working for us. You know how I had always joked 'our marriage was made in heaven, because we had no business doing it down here on earth?'

"Herman nodded with a wistful smile, "I remember. Some people were actually taking bets on how long it would last because you had such different personalities. I didn't take any of those bets but I was very curious myself. You really did have a temper in those days and she was so quiet and straight laced."

"You're right about the temper thing," I confessed. "The first year we were married we had a fight over something. I don't remember what the issue was but in frustration I yelled at her that she had better be careful or she just might get what she was asking for, as I slammed the drawer closed on a small student desk. I slammed it so hard the front panel split in half and fell to the floor. But much more damaging, a little orange, glass octopus I had bought for her on our honeymoon in Hawaii, fell off the desk and two of the legs were broken off. It scared her so much she dashed out of the apartment and went to see our pastor. She told him she was so afraid that she was going to leave me. Pastor Mees asked her if I had hit her. She said no. Pastor Mees then said, 'Go home to your husband!' Thankfully, she did. That was a close call. I nearly lost her and that would have been the biggest mistake of my life," I remembered remorsefully.

"You know, this is an area where your success as an athlete actually hurt you. It conditioned you to think everything was about you. I think the biggest change for you was when you began to realize that it wasn't," Herman recalled. "When you thought Gail's job was to make you happy, I remember there for a while, you could get pretty hot under the collar! I had always tried to point you toward scriptures such as, Proverbs 29:22, Ephesians 4:26 and James 1:19 so that you would calm down and become the husband you could and should be."

"I remember. Actually, looking back, we had a clue that it was going to work, when we went on the 'Newlywed Game' and won (see Appendix A-8). We had begun to think alike even that first year. You know, Gail and I never practiced Ephesians 4:26. It was a mistake but we used our own system. Although we went to bed angry many a night, and maybe even the next several nights, with some unresolved issue we eventually worked everything out and we suffered needlessly for this error.

Our system relied on an unwritten rule that seemed to take care of every disagreement. No matter how abused or misunderstood either of us felt it was more important to both of us to simply stay married than to win. Staying together was far more important than being right or coming out on top in any argument. And over the years, all the fights we had or crises we faced, all that garbage that can happen to a couple, glued us together even more tightly each time. So much so that when we had a big decision to make, both of us simply agreed on it or we flat out just didn't do it. If one or the other wasn't fully on board, it didn't happen. We never looked back and told the other one what we 'coulda, woulda or shoulda' have done.

"Over the years I would have my flare ups, but they got further and further apart and less and less violent. God has slowly but surely softened my heart. Last week when we talked about it, she said that it had become apparent to her that the more I studied the Bible, the less angry I became. And now she believes my anger has been replaced with compassion. I guess that explains it. All I know is that I am much happier now. I guess, 1 Corinthians 13:4–5 sums it up pretty much, 'love is patient, love is kind.' My job from now on is to encourage as many people as I can and to make sure Gail is happy that she 'went back home to her husband.'"

We both had a few errands to run before the formal reunion that evening and went our separate ways with promises to have a few "cold ones" later that night. Little did I know the surprise awaiting me that evening at the Sequoia Club in Buena Park. I ran my errands then went back to my Mom and Dad's house in Fullerton to get cleaned up and pick up Gail.

Later at the club Gail and I were beginning to worry about Herman and Gloria. When I finally saw Herman come into the ballroom my jaw hit the floor. He had a total stranger on his arm. It definitely was not Gloria. He hadn't said a word about his new companion when we met earlier that day. Where was Gloria? I had a very bad feeling and worried what this might mean? Had he gone off the deep end again? "Please, dear God, let this not be what I dread it is." She was wearing a beautiful, dark blue, brocade and very revealing dress that complimented every curve of her body and she seemed quite pleased with its affect on the room. She was flaunting it!

Herman introduced her, "This is Rachel. Rachel this is Gail and my best friend, Leroy."

After they sat down, I asked Herman to help me get some drinks for the girls. At the bar I laid into him, "What the h-e-double-1 is going on Herman? Where is Gloria? And where did Rachel come from?"

"Don't get all exorcised over it," he replied tersely. "Gloria and I are divorced. She was spending me into the poor house. And I met Rachel last night at the 601 Club (Gentleman's Club). We hit it off and she didn't have to work at the club tonight, so what the hey, here she is and I'm having fun for the first time in months."

I couldn't believe my ears but there was nothing to be gained beleaguering the point. "OK," I conceded. "I hope you know what you are doing." My head was spinning but I couldn't criticize him for the exact behavior I had been guilty of myself for so many years. I just hoped he would snap out of it, as I had eventually done myself.

However, bad went to worse. Herman went to the restroom and while he was gone Rachel got up and came around the table to my chair. She squatted down next to me making sure her neckline gapped open as she leaned forward ... way over toward me ... making sure I could see "everything" ... looked up with pleading eyes and asked me to dance. She was braless and both Gail and I could see a lot more of her bare body through the cavernous neckline than was comfortable for us to witness. Flummoxed, I got up and danced with her. I was sweating bullets by the time I got back to my chair. As we sat down Rachel looked coyly at Gail and told her she was a very lucky woman to have such a fine catch of a husband. Gail and I looked at each other, helpless what to do or say. Herman returned and the evening carried on. I felt like I was at "parade-rest" for the rest of the night. Every muscle in my body ached from the tension.

As the evening began to wind down, it was announced that anyone who wanted to could go down the hall to the bowling alley and roll a few lines, with no charge. Gail and I shot out the door and quickly found our shoes and bowling balls. We played a few of games with Gail scoring in the high nineties and low one hundreds. I did a little better at 115 to 123.

Herman and Rachel caught up to us and took the lane next to ours and began bowling. I rolled a 200 on my next game! Gail glared at me and almost wouldn't speak to me for the rest of the night. I couldn't convince her that Rachel had nothing to do with my sudden improvement.

However, I had a lot more to worry about than a jealous wife. Gail got over it in no time but Herman's behavior had serious implications and I had no idea how to help him. All those years when I had lived "loose and free" were now haunting me. I had no moral high ground from which to hold him accountable or even judge him. I could only pray and hope and be ready to encourage him to get off the "path to destruction" he was on.

My Way or The Highway?

"Teach me thy way, O Lord, and lead me in a plain path, because of mine enemies ... Wait on the Lord: be of good courage, and he shall strengthen thine heart: wait, I say, on the Lord." (Psalms 27:11 & 14)

The next day, after church, I met Herman at IHOP for a strawberry waffle and link sausages. It was like old times. Herman was dressed in slacks and a golf shirt and he seemed oblivious to the events of last night. He was in great spirits and smiling as if nothing had happened. I decided to let him bring it up when he was ready out of fear of backing him into a corner. We dove into our discussion routine as if we were back in San Diego.

"Leroy, I have a favor to ask," he opened up to me.

Quickly, I shot back, "I already have a roommate!"

Herman laughed so hard he almost spit out his coffee. "No, no, nothing like that," he assured me and then became very serious. "Yesterday, talking about the changes God was able to make in your life really hit a nerve for me," he stated in a very low and troubled voice. My heart began to race. What was about to happen undoubtedly would have deep and long lasting consequences.

"Leroy... I don't even know what I want to ask... but I'm in big trouble. I can't tell you all the details but I am in the middle of 'spiritual warfare,' he said with a shaky voice. 'I am at a fork in the road and the choices are really scary. Please pray for me like you have never prayed before! Someday, I will be able to share what's going on but I just can't do it right now."

I couldn't help but ask, "Can you tell me what area you are talking about? Does it have anything to do with Gloria... your law practice... your personal prayer life... are you in trouble with the law?"

"I don't want to say just now, but you are very close," was all he would share for the moment.

"Herman, remember how you counseled me at my crossroads? Is this anything like that?" My question was in reference to some midcareer decisions I had to make. "Remember my five year plan debacle, how I struck out at Solomon University? Then three years later out of another disastrous job, somehow God rescued me and I ended up at Biola (Bible Institute of Los Angeles)? Remember how you helped me with those decisions? Anything like that mess?"

The "mess" I referred to was in reference to my first coaching job. When I went to work at The California Institute of Technology in Pasadena (Caltech) as the head trainer and track coach in 1973 (one month after Gail and I were married). I had developed "MY PLAN." I would be at Caltech a maximum of five years. In that time, I would gain enough experience and connections to move up the coaching ladder to an NCAA, D-1 school. My personal success as an athlete all but assured me of a top job somewhere. But by my seventh year at Caltech I was puzzled, a little discouraged and starting to panic. I needed to expand my plan and become more proactive. I began to build a personal relationship with the AD (Athletic Director) at Solomon University a medium sized school with great facilities and recruiting possibilities. We would often meet for lunch and played a lot of golf together. We called each other frequently. He assured me that when an opening came along he would invite me to apply. In my eleventh year at Caltech he finally called. Was I still interested? If so, send my resume to him so he could publish the job search and no one would fit the job description better than I.

Feeling quite confident I applied for the job and "lo and behold" I was one of three finalists for the Track Coaching job at Solomon and there would be no trainer duties. Relieved, I thought to myself, finally, my plan is working and everything is starting to fall into place. My interview with the AD went very well (wink, wink). The University was in a great location and Gail and I began to make plans to buy a new house near the school.

However, a few weeks later I received an incredible letter from the Solomon search committee. "Dear Mr. Neal, thank you for applying but we have selected someone else. Good luck in your coaching career." Even more stunning, the person they selected was the same guy I had beat out for the job at Caltech. Herman saved me from going on a drinking binge of depression.

"Leroy, did you pray about this job?" Why in the world would I need to pray about it? I had MY PLAN!

"Did you turn it over to God and His plan for your life?"

"Oooops!"

After twelve years at Caltech I simply quit, without a job or any plans. I had decided it was a dead-end and I had to break out of the rut I was in. I began to work at "Paint, Patch and Repair" for local homeowners. I had a knack for this kind of work and by word of mouth recommendations from my clients I was never out of a job. I also took on a part-time job, coaching track at a local high school to keep my toe in the door for any new opportunities. But that job led nowhere. In fact, it blew up in my face. I had problems dealing with the other, part-time coaches who had been there for fifteen and twenty years and they had their own ways of doing things. They simply did not accept my leadership as the new "head coach." It got so bad that Herman and I began to meet after work, in the press box at the stadium to pray about it and discuss what to do. He was temporarily living in the area, while representing one of his clients in a big political lawsuit. It was reminiscent of our San Diego routine and for the next several weeks we met regularly in the press box at the school stadium. We read and discussed a couple of books on how to make a wise decision using Biblical principles.

Finally, one day I gave up. I had had enough. I told Herman that apparently God wanted me to be rich, not happy. At long last, I would submit to His will. I was going to give up coaching and begin building apartment buildings and become filthy rich. Herman was envious of the clarity and finality of my decision. I had a wealth of experience in construction from working with my contractor-father and was finally at peace about my personal career.

However, when I got home that night, the red light message button on my phone was blinking. I pushed the button and heard Dr. Roger Soule, the Athletic Director at BIOLA (Bible Institute of Los Angeles) University, inviting me to apply for the Track Coaching job there. They had been searching for a new coach for more than two years and a friend had given the search committee my name. A few weeks later, I was in fact, the new head track coach of the BIOLA Eagles. It is pretty obvious in retrospect; my submission was key to "receiving" my heart's desire. I had not "received because I had not asked" believing. There was that blasted mustard seed again!

Back at IHOP, his eyes on the floor, Herman slowly shook his head, "Something like that . . . but much worse!"

Immediately I closed my eyes and thought a prayer. "God in heaven, Creator of everything, watch over this man who has done so much for me and I love him for it but I am fearful that I am about to lose him, Amen."

"Well, how 'bout that Ryder Cup. The US won by one point." Herman had suddenly changed the subject. I just stared blankly back at him. He had moved on and the serious stuff was over, so I brought up something that had been troubling me.

Why Didn't We Know That?

Nicodemus said to Him, "How can these things be?" Jesus answered and said to him, "Are you the teacher of Israel and do not understand these things?" (John 3:9–10)

The Kosovo War had brought out, arguably the most esoteric discussion about armed conflicts in the history of our country. The United States was fighting a war in a foreign land to defend Muslims. All that Herman had ever told me about Islam cried out the incongruity of this action. The big question was, where in our glorious past was there less American interest at stake, less to be gained with such an action? Oh, yes, lots of politicians piled on with all the usual arguments about human rights and worldwide condemnations of Mulosevic's evil acts. Apparently, killing babies in the womb does not qualify as a human rights violation and the silence of those same people was deafening when Christians were beheaded, disemboweled, chopped to pieces and lit on fire in hundreds of other locations all over the world. The lack of engagement over these despicable acts screamed the obvious hypocrisy of the political elite.

More importantly, at least for me, it also brought out, front and center, how little we knew about Islam here at home. Herman had always taught me how fundamentalist Muslims think about the rest of the world. Sharia Law was their bedrock goal, attained any way, at any cost, and there was no flexibility in Islamic politics and theology. Islam is not in the least bit secretive about it's methods to attain a world wide Caliphate. Open war, terrorism, subterfuge or attrition are all approved strategies as explained in the Koran and demonstrated over and over by Muhammad, himself. But absolutely no one in the US was talking about it. It was an abstract subject with no affect on our daily lives. And the Christian community as well seemed totally unprepared to discuss any honest comparisons?

"Herman, I have just got to ask, why in the world are Americans so dead-headed and refuse to see what is right in front of them?" For myself, personal laziness was partly to blame and the remoteness of the war was disarming as well. Flat out, I had neglected to be "in the Word" in a serious way for way too long which left me unprepared for such a discussion. I am reminded of that neglect every morning when I get up and pass through the living room where Gail is seated, studying her daily devotions. She almost never misses her morning feeding. But there has to be more to it than just a lackadaisical approach by the American people. "What is it?" I pleaded.

Herman never beat around the bush on any topic. He was succinct as usual, "PC (Political Correctness)!"

"That's it? Is it that simple?" I wondered.

He broadened his answer. "Many Americans think all religions are pretty much the same. They generally look at religion as nothing more than a public moral code of conduct or as some branch of philosophy. With this sense of equivalence there can be no judgmentalism between religions. There are no absolutes and present day PC intimidates honest debate about such questions. Not only does it roadblock discussion, it has also warped the very definition of key words necessary for those discussions," he continued. "I truly shudder at the way words such as "tolerance" and "dialogue" have been reduced to silly dribble. At one time, tolerance meant allowing others to have a different opinion. Not so now. Tolerance now means that you cannot even challenge currently 'correct' opinions without being branded as a radical and too extreme for polite society to boot. You must now 'tolerate' and live by the minority opinion. Dialogue used to mean a discussion between parties of differing views in an attempt to understand the beliefs of each other. That has changed! It now means you must validate and agree with the politically protected group's worldview or you will be branded as a rigid 'right wing nut' or 'Islamophobic' hater.

"Even the term 'radical' has become a weapon rather than a descriptive word. The media uses 'radical' when they do not like or don't agree with someone, to convey the message that particular person is bad or evil or simply 'out of touch.' All to often, that 'out of touch' group or person is any Christian that attempts to hold politicians to even basic levels of accountability. The double standard bombards us from newspapers, TV reports and public forums," he explained.

"When words lose their meaning, communication, let alone debate is no longer possible. C.S. Lewis was well aware of this danger. In his book, *Studies in Words,* he describes the nature of language and its role in developing reasoned and objective inquiry and warns against their degradation. 'But the greatest cause of verbicide is the fact that most people are obviously far more anxious to express their approval and disapproval of things than to describe them. Hence the tendency of words to become less descriptive and more evaluative;...'[1] PC gleefully trades such lofty thinking for the practical achievement of political ends regardless of the cost," Herman concluded.

"That seems to be pretty much, right on," I agreed. "I've noticed that recent violent events by Fundamental Islamists have been excused because those involved had been 'radicalized' and the implied assumption is that they did not represent true, peaceful, Islam. America has done something to set that radical off like a ticking time bomb. It's our fault for making them so angry."

Herman added, shaking his head, "That's just another PC dodge. Those **radicals and ISIS are Islam,** in the most basic and fundamental way! Not to see that is total naiveté. The mainstream media and the PC police simply stick their heads into the sand and ignore what is right in front of them. The reason those radicals do the things they do is because, we are not Muslims! **WE ARE INFIDELS!!!** The only thing we could possibly do to deflect their violent acts . . . would be to become Muslim ourselves! Their goal is a world wide Caliphate, by any means, at any cost!

"The media is simply incapable of accepting that 'moderate' Muslims, really aren't Muslim. To be a moderate Muslim they have to turn your back on two thirds of the very foundation (the Sira and Hadith) of true Islam and make up their own rules the rest of the way. If Christians were to turn their backs to any part of the Bible or any aspect of what we know about Jesus, we might be able to claim some sort of lofty and universal moral ground but would have to admit, we certainly are not Christians. In this environment, the very thing that is needed most (talking to each other) becomes the least welcome and least honest component of our society."

Herman summarized, "The unfortunate outcome of paralysis by PC is that many, if not most, Americans have never heard an honest discussion comparing Islam to Christianity. It would seem the Playground Bully has been replaced by the PC Police. In this vacuum, outrageous misconceptions often are the rule rather than the exception, which is where all this nonsense about Islam being a "peaceful" religion comes from."

I have to admit to my own biases in this area and had therefore set my sights on the discovery of "facts" rather than opinions for my book. This is the environment I would operate in as I began the search for answers to my questions. Understanding PC and my own irresponsibility by no means is an excuse for not knowing what I should have known and would have known, with the "right tools." Fortunately, I eventually completed my research. The results of all that reading and the many discussions with Herman helped me answer my six questions.

However, in light of Herman's behavior at the reunion, I had new questions. Where was he headed, personally and spiritually? Rachel's appearance worried me to no end. His personal conduct seemed to be veering all over the place and it did not bode well. Our parallel lives appeared to once again be headed in opposite directions.

Chapter 6

MY JOURNEYS END

—————— ✳ ——————

"Who's on first, What's on second . . ."

"For in the case of those who have once been enlightened and have tasted of the heavenly gift and have been made partakers of the Holy Spirit . . . and then have fallen away, it is impossible to renew them again to repentance, since they again crucify to themselves the Son of God, and put Him to open shame." (Hebrews 6:4 & 6)

Wednesday, Jan. 7, 2015, 12:30 PM, Denver International Airport: The noise and chaos of the Frontier Air Line terminal is the worst I have ever experienced. Finding a place to sit had been a major project in itself. When I finally found a seat half way back to the lobby, I sat down and tried to read. Unable to concentrate on my book I glanced up and down the corridor and did a double take of a gentleman sitting five seats down, to my right. He looked vaguely familiar but had turned away too quickly for me to get a good look at his face. It was downright eerie how his body language reminded me of someone but I couldn't quite place it. And then it came to me. But that was impossible! This guy was way too thin to be the person I was thinking of. And he was dressed too absurdly. He was wearing some kind of a middle-eastern robe, leather sandals and no socks. His hair was long and grey and unkempt. He appeared to have a beard destined for the Guinness Book of World Records.

It was as if Herman Reyhadi had vaporized into thin air without a clue that he had ever existed. He had simply disappeared without a farewell, a phone call or even a note. It just didn't make sense and was spooky how we lost contact. We had always hooked up for our high school reunions and called each other at least every two or three months to catch up on our lives and discuss world events, politics and especially religion.

But the way this guy hunched his shoulders was just too much for my curiosity. Those shoulders were a definite "tell." I got up and pretended to get a drink of water. When I started back to my seat I met a pair of coal black eyes boring holes through me.

"How you doing Leroy?"

It **WAS** Herman, my best friend in high school and for more than fifty years in all! "What in the world are you doing here? Where the hell have you been for the last 16 years? Why are you dressed like this? Is Rachel with you?" My questions came in rapid fire without waiting for answers!

He just sat there calm and cool until I ran down. "I'm stuck here just like you," he pointed out.

I began to grill him, "Why did you drop out on me, Herman? No phone call, no letter, I had no idea how to find you and you sit there cool as a cucumber and say Hi Leroy, how are you doing?" I was awash in emotions. Why had Herman abandoned me? Memories flashed through my mind. Herman and I had shared so much over the years. It was incomprehensible that he had completely disappeared. For all I knew, he was dead. And now, here he was, looking like a homeless bum.

My thoughts and emotions ran the gamut from relief and elation to anger and frustration. I didn't have a clue "who was on first or what was on second . . ." I needed some answers! I traded seats with the person next to Herman and settled in for his explanations.

He started with a word of caution. "I may have to leave suddenly. Don't try to follow me. Promise me you won't say anything to anyone about meeting me here today. I have been in a lot of trouble and ... certain people ... are probably looking for me." Flabbergasted, I could only nod that I understood even though I didn't have the "foggiest" what this meant.

"A lot of things happened to me after moving out from your apartment in San Diego

and even more so after our fortieth reunion. Big things! Life-changing things! Things that are going to be very hard for you to believe or even understand! Rachel isn't with me because we never got married. We lived together for about three years but she was running around on me and I just packed up and left. Apparently marriage counseling is not one of my strong suits. Where I've been, I can't tell you and it is best you just don't know. I'm dressed this way because I now follow Allah. I have converted to Islam."

BAM! BAM! BAM! It was as if I had been hit three times with a baseball bat. Staggered, I managed to gasp, "This can't be. How in the world did all that happen?"

Herman leaned in close so that our conversation was as private as possible under the circumstances. He was almost whispering. "I know that you are going to be disappointed but the truth is I have been in one bad situation after another to the point that I lost faith in Christianity. It just didn't have any answers for what

I was going through. Two divorces and one shack-up mistake were bad enough, but then I went to jail for five years because my partners in the law firm threw me under the bus. I had signed some papers I shouldn't have signed and ended up taking the blame for some bribery charges against a couple of politicians. I can't tell you who they are or what offices they held for fear of going back to jail.

"While I was in jail, I was raped and beat up several times. All of my so-called friends abandoned me. I never told you because I was too ashamed. My money ran out paying other lawyers to do what I used to do. Once I was out of jail I had nothing. I was desperate and committed a couple of robberies just to have food and a place to sleep. I went back to jail for those crimes. But this time I met some Muslims who befriended me. They gave me purpose and a target for my anger. And I can tell you that my anger was and still is monumental. I had been Mr. 'Goody-Two-Shoes' for decades and look what it got me."

I couldn't take any more and yelled, **"Stop it! You have got to be putting me on!"** This was the guy who had nurtured me, preached to me and encouraged me for more than thirty years on how I should give my life to Jesus. Without Herman I doubt I would have ever become a Christian.

"Did this have anything to do with 'research' in Palestine? And why did you say Palestine instead of Gaza or the Occupied Territories or the West Bank or even Israel?" I wanted to know.

"Please don't ask about that. I simply can't honestly answer," he deferred, "but I can tell you that I have not been involved in any fighting. I was too old and they turned me down as a handicap to them on any battlefield. I was much more valuable in a totally different way. That's all I can say."

"OK, then at least tell me..." I stopped in mid-sentence, gripped by an outlandish thought. **Herman! This is a God thing!** Meeting you here today is more than providential. It was ordained!" I was close to shouting. "You have no idea what I'm talking about, but it is just mind blowing. All those years that you coddled me and gently brought me along until I finally, really, truly believed in Jesus and now ... our roles are reversed! Now I have to share some things with you and hope they make a difference. Listen, your situation, evolution, transformation or whatever you want to call it, fits like a glove with something I experienced only four days ago!"

"Calm down!" Herman hissed. "Don't draw attention to us, for crying out loud!" "OK! OK! OK!" I slowed the tempo and lowered the volume. "Last Sunday I was sitting in church and the pastor gave a sermon on the Riches of God. About half way through he cited Acts 9:4–5, the conversion of Saul on the road to Damascus. Herman, I had never considered how radical that was. Ever since I became a Christian in 1973 I have attended hundreds of Bible studies and came to Acts 9 uncountable times."

"I believe I led some of those studies," Herman smirked.

"Yes you did which only makes this even more ironic," I countered. "The point is that whole experience there in church last Sunday snowballed into two incredible journeys. But most outrageous of all, it brought me face to face with three radical Muslims who were a lot like what you have just told me about yourself."

Herman just stared blankly back at me. I needed to make a better connection of how it related to him. "I'm pretty sure you will know who I'm talking about." I explained my flashes of insight on Sunday, the three Muslims I had remembered from media headlines and how I thought about my insecurity because of my non-dramatic conversion.

"Herman, I have been reading and researching and praying, the way you taught me, until I'm exhausted. And the more I pray about these things the more God has revealed to me about Islam and radical conversions and just about everything. I feel so great! I have been freed from years of self-doubt. I had been guilty of living in a bubble. I had way too many giants that were entirely too small. I had just about dried up and quit living my faith. I felt powerless.

"Iron sharpens iron but without you around I had lost my sharpener to bounce things off of. That's no excuse but I was withdrawing because I didn't have to face any real or serious challenges. Chris Nichols described my condition to a tee, 'Our whole world becomes filled with others just like us. There comes a point where we no longer know anyone who isn't a Christian. We withdraw into the Christian world (bubble) that is created around us and we have less and less contact with the people Jesus loves.'[1] The challenge of that sermon four days ago shook me up and got the juices flowing again. My personal conversion has been renewed and expanded or at least I understand it better. I felt the Holy Spirit begin to move in me again. Suddenly, I was ready to 'do something' although it wasn't all that clear what 'something' might entail. And now, here you are. You are one of those people Jesus loves. And it's my turn to pray for you the way you did for me all those years."

Herman's jaw muscles were clinched and knotted as if he were chewing on a tuff piece of meat. His stare went right through me. I had seen that look only once before, when his mother died. Our roles, our lives our very selves had traded places and it was my turn to try to get him back on the "straight and narrow." My first hope was to change his heart but I sensed it was already frozen from his look of resolve. The next best strategy was to compare Islam and Christianity from a practical and logical perspective. I thought a quick, private prayer and charged in.

What It Is and What It Ain't

*"For vexation slays the foolish man, and anger
kills the simple ... His sons are far from safety,
they are even oppressed in the gate." (Job 5:2, 4)*

Herman's face softened and he gave me a wan smile, "So, the student exceeds the teacher? Leroy, your efforts are appreciated and I am really quite proud of you. It won't change anything but for what it's worth quoting Job was probably your best chance to change my mind. Of all the scriptures, I can certainly identify with him more than anyone or anything else you might have used. It seems to me that you have indeed become pretty good at finding the 'right tools.'"

I replied, "I understand, but for the sake of discussion, which you have always jumped on in the past, and for old times sake, let me practice a reasoned argument ... for the next Muslim I might meet." I was hoping our long friendship still meant enough to continue, even if it was only an intellectual exercise.

He indulged me and nodded, "OK professor. Give me your best shot."

"Herman, you have taught me so much about Islam already. I realize that I won't be able to tell you anything you don't already know about Muslims. But I do think I have had some pretty good, if not original revelations," I began, anticipating a factual counter-argument. "And, apparently it is too late to use 2 Peter 3:17, 'be on your guard lest, being carried away by the error of unprincipled men, you fall from your own steadfastness' because I'm thinking that your becoming Muslim had less to do with being led astray than your being given a platform to act out your own previous decision."

Herman agreed, "That's 'one in a row' for you Leroy. You're pretty close."

I continued, "Well, if your mind was already made up, you didn't need any additional knowledge. And I probably don't need to elaborate how Islam and Christianity

are the two largest religions in the world because they both embrace the same idea, from opposite perspectives, different from all other religions."

"So what is that idea, oh learned one?" Herman continued to humor me.

"It's very simple. Most other religions concentrate on self-improvement or control. The 'deity,' if you will, is already in you and only needs to be realized and identified. Islam and Christianity concentrate on a relationship, with God as the ultimate controller. The difference is Christians see it as similar to a father/child, positive, love relationship and they take responsibility for their own condition. Islam's view is one of a citizen to a policeman with a negative relationship and no room to make a mistake and they tend to blame others for their problems."

"That's close enough for me," Herman continued to play along.

Feeling more confident, I tried to expand on the differences, "Then would you agree that they also differ in that Christianity is based on grace and seeks to do good and improve things versus seeking domination by force? And it operates from love of God versus blind obedience out of fear and participates in the relationship with assurance of salvation versus works related rituals and obedience because Allah says so, with no way of knowing the outcome except as a martyr? Does that sound like a fair comparison?"

Herman's answer was stunning, "Yes, that just about sums it up."

I had expected a strong push back and was stalled for the moment.

"Anything else?" he prompted me.

Pulling myself together I next asked, "Then why in the world did you join up with them (Muslims)?"

Herman never participated in half-thoughts or arguing for the sake of argument. He got straight to the heart of his situation. "There really isn't that much to it Leroy. I know everything I need to know. I have no unanswered questions. Anger is enough for me right now. I don't kid myself about Islam or an afterlife or that Islam is some kind of big cure for anything except my rage. Islam gives me the cover I need to break things!"

His matter of fact response had me back on my heels. I recalled the enlightenment I once received from a psychologist. "Emotions are not right or wrong ... they just are (exist)!" It was clear that discussion, reasoning or even begging would have no effect.

Bargaining for time to collect my thoughts on how to respond, I excused myself to visit the restroom where I did indeed have an urgent need to let out some of the many cups of coffee I had consumed during the delays. At 73 years of age, I never strayed too far from a restroom.

Herman had surprised me with the complete acceptance of my analysis of the Christian versus Islam comparison. He was not blinded by rage ... he was focused and calculating because of it. Suddenly I felt a wave of nausea sweep over me. There was a knot in my stomach the size of a basketball. A brutal thought hit me. Herman had demonstrated over and over again that he knew everything there was to know ABOUT Jesus ... but did he ever KNOW Jesus? It was the only explanation that made sense to me of how he could possibly have become a Muslim. My heart sank as I tried not to believe he could know everything there was to know about Islam and still convert simply because he wanted revenge. If it were true, all those years of his witnessing to me would be blown to smithereens.

I finished my business in the restroom and privately prayed for wisdom as I returned to my seat. Herman's chair was empty! He had left without so much as an "adios" just like he had done in 1999. I closed my eyes and pleaded, "Dear God in heaven, what can I do? If there is anything at all in your great plan that will bring him to his senses, do it now. Please 'renew a right spirit within him.' Let him know how much you love him."

Over the next few weeks and months there were many reports about ISIS and other radical Muslim activities. My attention was drawn specifically to the new ways they were communicating

188

their plans through encryption and social media, to shoot down airplanes and attack large, soft targets. The number of incidents seemed to be increasing and in multiple areas around the world. Most notable were the attacks in Paris and Belgium but there were hot spots, seemingly everywhere. I listened closely to those reports trying to determine if Herman might be involved. Nothing specific ever materialized and I never heard from him or about him again.

Outside the snow had stopped. Flight 405 to LAX had finally arrived at 10:30 PM. I boarded the plane as late as I could, all the time looking around, just in case. It was an empty exercise. Herman had disappeared again and I was left with an even emptier feeling of a lost opportunity. "Dear God, I give him up into your mercy and I thank you for the years you gave me with him. It made all the difference. Amen." I reluctantly let him go. "Good-bye my brother. I have loved you like no other man I have ever known."

EPILOGUE

Answers

"As we have said before, so I say again now, if
any man is preaching to you a gospel contrary
to that which you received, let him be accursed."
(Gal. 1:9)

R emembering my fifty-six year journey following high school, although tedious at times turned out to be more than informative. It was exciting, fun and quite nostalgic as it armed me with knowledge and a sense of self-worth. The long trek through my past life resulted in more growth and understanding than the previous seventy-three years combined. I now had a better perspective of my role in God's protracted drama and I had found the answers to my questions as well.

But incredibly more important, the Bible had come alive and vibrant for me. It was no longer simply an historical document composed of moral rules to live by. The focus was no longer in the past. It now represented the past, the present and the future. It had become my comfort food as I communed in relationship with God. I now felt that I was in 'homeostatic' heaven and my search for answers was satisfied... for the moment.

1. Is there a significant difference between Islam and Christianity? If so, how are they different?

Islam: It is an authoritative religion based on strict obedience and does not tolerate questioning, original thought or open discussion. The greatest sin is not to be obedient to and love of Allah. Apostasy is the second greatest sin, often punishable by death. It is a works and ritual oriented community in which good works earn salvation but there is no scale to determine how many works are enough. Women have virtually no rights, inherit half as much as males (Koran 4:11–12) and their testimony in court is worth one half that of a man. And in cases of rape, the woman is quite often punished, sometimes even executed by her own family as though it was her fault and she had brought dishonor to the family. There is absolutely no assurance of salvation except as a martyr, although some sins can be made up for by additional ritual participation. Islam's goal is world domination by Caliphate, to be achieved by open war, attrition, terrorism or subterfuge.

The Koran is the holy book and provides an outline for Islam. It is explained and interpreted through the Sira and the Hadith but Muhammad not the Koran is the personification of Islam. The Koran features 114 chapters called Surah arranged by size, in more or less descending order, beginning with the longest and ending with the shortest. There is no time line or subject order. There is no beginning, middle or end in the Surah or in the Koran as a whole, with one exception. It is characterized by thousands of independent statements with no apparent theme although there are groupings of related statements. Islam considers the Koran to be revealed messages from Allah through the angel Gabriel to Muhammad over a 23-year period and written down over the years but there were no eyewitnesses to these revelations. At one time there were several competing versions (3 or 4 popular ones). The one favored by those in power was finally canonized and the others were destroyed around 650 AD.

Christianity: It is a grace-based, love relationship. The Christian willingly does good works as a response to the gift of salvation. Salvation is possible only through the blood of Jesus Christ, who died on the cross to pay for our sins and through this act renews a direct relationship for us with God. The goal of every Christian is summed up in the "great commission," to preach the Gospel until every person on earth has heard it and has an opportunity to be saved. Healthy Christian churches welcome debate, discussion and questioning of all sermons, doctrinal statements and scriptural passages.

The Christian Bible features an Old Testament (before Jesus) with 39 books and a New Testament (about the life of Jesus through Revelation) with 27 books. Genesis through Job is presented in chronological order. Subsequent books become topically arranged until you get to the Minor Prophets that again are somewhat in chronological order. The New Testament is pretty much on a time line of order also. Each book has a beginning, middle and end as it reveals messages from God. There were forty, inspired by God, authors and they completed their writings over a fifteen hundred year period. The New Testament was canonized in 170 AD and the entire Bible as we know it today was canonized about 397 AD. As a whole, the meaning of the Bible rests on Jesus and his work of salvation.

2. Is there evidence that the Koran and the Bible are essentially the same or strikingly different in unity, prophecy,

inerrancy and understandability? Can either stand alone without supplemental references or commentaries?

Unity in the Koran: The Surah in the Koran are a collection of unrelated statements with no order or timeline and are arranged more or less by size. There is no beginning, middle or end in the Surah or the Koran as a whole except for the story of Joseph. There are few apparent themes other than multiple directives about rituals, works and other things to do or avoid. There are multiple early references to peaceful directives but they are usually abrogated by later violent revelations from Muhammad. The only clear themes are to spill the blood and plunder anyone who is not Muslim and the assurance of salvation as a martyr.

Unity of the Bible: It is a harmonious and continuous story, from Genesis to Revelation, revealing the true nature of God. It is a progressive story with each book building on the previous one. Each book and the Bible as a whole tell this story with a beginning a middle and an end in each case. Miracles and prophecies tie the individual books and the Bible itself together as a complete revelation from God.

Prophecy in the Koran: Most of the statements approaching prophecy appear to be suspicious rewordings of Biblical texts or outright plagiarisms.

Prophecy in the Bible: There are more than 300 prophecies in the Old Testament that are accurately fulfilled in the New Testament. These prophecies are usually made by a religious leader but sometimes they come directly from God. Some examples of these prophesies are Mica predicting Jesus will be born in Bethlehem, Isaiah talks about the "virgin birth," Zechariah describes the "King" riding on the foal of a donkey and David details the crucifixion in his Psalms, 900 years before it happens.

Inerrancy of the Koran: There were several competing Korans in the middle 650s of different lengths, with some Surah missing in certain versions and others in contradiction. Many errors are also found in the current Koran, ranging from misinformed explanations concerning Developmental Biology, dates of certain historical events and the locations for some of those events, plus five contradictory explanations about the creation of man in addition to errors in Arabic grammar.

Inerrancy in the Bible: Muslims will claim the many versions of the Bible (RSV, AS, KJ, etc.) are proof of errors and contradictions. There are no errors, only variations in translations. The theology, doctrine and messages are consistent and true in all translations. With forty different authors, over fifteen hundred years in the writing, all in harmony and supporting each other is a powerful argument for one story, without error. Every challenge about various verses, dates, times and named kings, has been answered and disproved by respected authorities.

Understandability of the Koran: The Koran cannot be understood on its own. The Sira and Hadith are required to explain Koranic principles and directives. This is because Muhammad is the personification of Islam and the Koran is unknowable except through the examples set by the Prophet, himself. Contributing to the confusion, there are several accepted Sira and Hadith (4 to 5 each), featuring many sets of volumes the size of standard dictionaries. Their lines of cross-references are very complex and it takes an Islamic scholar to sort them out into understandable messages.

Understandability of the Bible: Any normal person can pick up the Bible and begin reading any of the 66 books, with the possible exception of Revelation and immediately understand the story. The protagonist and the antagonist will be recognized very quickly. With a minimal effort, themes, prophecies and core messages will soon be recognized.

3. What are the dynamics of "radical" conversions in both religions? What are the unmet needs that lead to conversion in both cases?

Radical Islam: News media stories about crimes committed by "radical" Muslims have several common elements. A large number of the radical converts to Islam have histories of anger, disenfranchisement and often one or more previous cases of illegal activities or even incarcerations. Black Americans, as a group have the highest rate of radical conversion. Other "radical" incidents involve already Muslim individuals who display "Fundamentalist" backgrounds. That is, they accept a fundamental interpretation of the Koran, the Sira and the Hadith, which promote violent acts in the name of Allah. As a group these radicals display highly emotional reactions to any challenge or debate over their motivations or the goals of Islam. Their emotional journey is one from a peaceful demeanor to anger and ending in destructive behavior. They realize they are broken and want to break things out of revenge toward others. They believe their problems have been caused by others. They are radical in the sense that their behavior is dramatically violent and unacceptable.

Radical Christians: They begin their journey with destructive behavior, move to a peaceful demeanor and graduate to constructive behavior. These individuals express their brokenness by trying to put the pieces back together. They accept responsibility for the problems they have and set out to change in a positive manner. They are only radical in the sense that they are very public and dramatic in their conversion. They have become "dramatically" different in attitude and positive behavior.

4. Is Islam truly a "religion of peace"? Is Christianity more militant and violent than commonly professed or admitted?

Islam: Fundamental Islam has always been and continues to be constantly at war with anyone or any country that does not accept Sharia law and become Muslim. "Moderate" Muslims can only be moderate by ignoring fundamental, holy texts from the Islamic Trilogy. The unapologetic goal of Fundamental Islam is world domination at any cost and by any means.

Christianity: Historically there have been many examples of violence in the name of God. However, those examples did not wear the mantel of true Christian doctrine. Use of the "sword" in the name of Christianity is anathema to the teachings of Jesus. The goal of true Christianity is to win the heart and mind of every person on earth through a loving and sacrificial message of hope and salvation, by persuasion and example

5. Was my non-dramatic conversion as powerful as more radical/dramatic Christian conversions?

My conversion: My conversion was indeed as powerful as any other. The fact that I did not understand this at first was a reflection of my insecurity and lack of using it as it was intended. I am convinced of this after studying the comparison of St. Augustine and C.S. Lewis. In the process of writing this book I have felt a new, stronger sense of the Holy Spirit enabling me to step out in confidence and faith.

6. **Why was I so unprepared to rationally discuss these comparisons with my counterpart, a sincere Muslim?**

My unpreparedness: I felt overwhelmed and unprepared for two reasons. First, I must acknowledge my lackadaisical and lazy attitude toward living a life of faith and especially studying the word of God more regularly and in greater depth. Second, I believe that current political correctness lulls us to sleep and smothers our natural curiosity and willingness to talk about sensitive things. I plan to do something about this in my own life. How about you?

Perspectives

"Not that I have already obtained it, or have already become perfect, but I press on in order that I may lay hold of that for which also I was laid hold of by Christ Jesus" (Phil.3:12)

This book is not, nor was it ever intended to be of textbook quality discussing the politically sensitive issues of Islam vs. Christianity. I defer to the many excellent theologians and apologists when wrestling with the complicated aspects of conversion, radical or not. This effort was only one man's journey to understand himself and a few others, not a compelling argument for any particular position. Further, motivation for writing this book should not be confused with any noble goal. I had simply recognized that part of my faith was beginning to dry up and leave a dead space inside me. This scared me because it seemed to be growing. Pastor Hall's sermon awakened a hunger in me to know more, to be more, even as I begin my ascent into eternity. I needed a project to help me begin to grow again, intellectually and spiritually. As a result, although I did not feel compelled to charge out the door to "change the world," I did recognize the importance of becoming more active and intentional, living and expressing my faith on a daily basis.

Carrots or Billy Clubs

"Though I am free and belong to no man, I make myself a slave to everyone, to win as many as possible ... I have become all things to all men so that by all possible means I might save some." *(1 Corinthians 9:19, 23)*

I began this effort out the feeling of being at a disadvantage in any discussion comparing Islam to Christianity. I hope the reader has learned as much as I have. However, I must vigorously caution everyone about how they handle this information. It would be catastrophic to use this newfound knowledge as a weapon against any Muslim we may come in contact with. The Muslim world will not become "Christianized" by physical force or even force of argument but by loving those "whom Jesus loves."

In Summary

"Consider it all joy, my brethren, when you encounter various trials. Knowing that the testing of your faith produces endurance. And let endurance have its perfect result, that you may be perfect and complete, lacking nothing." (James 1:2–4)

Retracing the steps of my faith journey was scary, fun and reinvigorating and I learned incredible things about Islam in the process. It breathed new life into an "older man" who needed a kick in the pants. When Socrates said, "The unexamined life is not worth living." he had talked his fellow Greeks into sentencing him to death for the heresy of questioning current, politically correct beliefs. The consequences of reexamining my own life did not carry such a grave outcome but it did give me the frame of reference that all lives have value even if we do not immediately recognize it. Everyone should reexamine their own lives to confirm that God does not make junk.

My feelings and thoughts are well summed up by David Limbaugh, "I give all the thanks and glory to Jesus Christ, but there simply are no words sufficient to communicate it. I know however, that He knows the depth of my gratitude for *everything,* including pursuing me, not giving up on me, forgiving me, and dying on the cross for me."[1]

And now my next journey begins.

APPENDIX A

1. Visiting Mom in California

2. Sunset League Champions
(six seniors and one freshman)

SETS RECORD — Leroy Neal is shown above, winning mile at Southern Cal championship meet Saturday night in Bakersfield. He was timed in 4:09.2, for a new meet mark. At left is teammate Harry McCalla, who holds national record at 4:09.0. Both run this Saturday in state finals at Modesto.

3. (three individual national records and 9 combined national relay records)

Dahl 'Foul' Crucial

Oxy Kayos UCLA

Sunday, April 15, 1962   CCC   Los Angeles Herald Examiner

By Ralph Alexander

4.

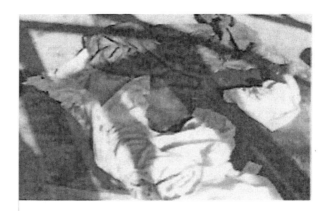

5. Eli hut in Viet Nam

6. Our Colorado family

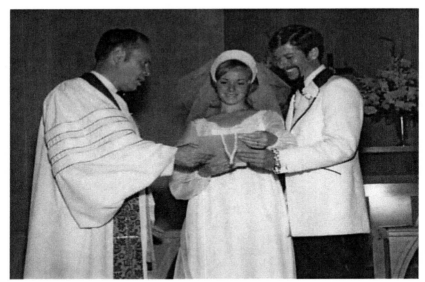

7. August 25, 1973 with Pastor Mees

8. Newlywed Game winners— 1973

APPENDIX B

Bible and Koran verses compared

The following is a partial list of scriptural comparisons between the Bible and the Koran. The similarities are obvious and argue that much of the Koran was Muhammad's effort to restate Biblical principles, directives and theological positions. He believed the Jews and Christians of his time had missed God's true intent and had bastardized the Holy Scriptures. The Koran is an attempt to clarify and further interpret the true messages from God. He repeatedly states that the Book (Bible) was God inspired, including the New Testament (Injeel). He did not set out to replace the Bible but to better interpret it and produce a similar holy book for the Arab world. His biggest complaint was that he disagreed with the Christians when they added Jesus and the Holy Spirit to God, which to him was blasphemous polytheism.

The King James Version of the Bible is quoted in these comparisons in an effort to use the most similar sounding words and phrases. Because of the volume of comparisons, only one or two Bible verses are compared per Surah and only a representative sample of Surah are be included. This list demonstrates a pattern whereby the Koran is basically a collection of restatements of the Bible. There are some divergent and original messages, but there are no new, complete stories or narratives in the Koran. There are statements about Abraham, Moses, Isaac, Jacob, John the Baptist, and Jesus. But there is no beginning, middle, and end to any of these stories, except in the case of Joseph.

Sura I:4 **"Thee only do we worship, and to thee do we cry for help."**

Mt. 4:10 "For it is written, Thou shalt worship the Lord thy God, and him only shalt thou serve."

Heb. 13:6 "The Lord is my helper, and I will not fear what man shall do unto me."

Sura I:5, 6 **"Guide thou us on the straight path, the path of those to whom Thou has been gracious ..."**

Ps. 27:11 "Teach me your way, O Lord; lead me in a straight path ..."

Pr. 3:6 "In all thy ways acknowledge him, and he shall direct thy paths."

Sura II:5 "Their hearts and their ears hath God sealed up; and over their eyes is a covering."

Jer. 5:21 "Hear now this, O foolish people, and without understanding; which have eyes and see not; which have ears and hear not."

1 Cor. 2:9 "But it is written, Eye hath not seen, nor ear heard, neither have entered into the heart of man, the things which God hath prepared for them that love him."

Sura I:41 "Will ye enjoin what is right upon others, and forget yourselves?"

Mt. 7:4 "Or how wilt thou say to thy brother, Let me pull out the mote that is in thine eye, but considerest not the beam that is in thine own eye?"

Luke 6:42 "Thou hypocrite, cast out first the beam out of thine own eye, and then shalt thou see clearly to pull out the mote that is in thy brother's eye."

Sura III:5 "And I have come to attest the Law which was before me ..."

Mt. 5:17 "Do not think that I have come to abolish the Law or the Prophets; I have not come to abolish them but to fulfill them."

Gal. 3:24–26 "Wherefore the law was our schoolmaster to bring us unto Christ, that we might be justified by faith. But after that faith is come, we are no longer under a schoolmaster. For ye are children of God by faith in Christ Jesus."

Sura III:161 "They said with their lips what was not in their hearts! But God Knoweth what they concealed,..."

Isa. 29:13 "The Lord says, "These people come near to me with their mouth And honor me with their lips, but their hearts are far from me."

Mt. 15:8 "This people draweth nigh unto me with their mouth, and honoreth me with their lips; but their heart is far from me."

Sura IV:42 "And for those who bestow their substance in alms to be seen of men, and believe not in God and in the Last Day."

Mt. 6:1,2 "Take heed that ye do not your alms before men, to be seen of them when thou doest thine alms, do not sound a trumpet before thee, as the hypocrites do in the synagogues and in the streets, that they may have glory of men."

Sura VII:62 "But they treated him (Noah) as a liar: so We delivered him and those who were with him in the Ark, and We drowned those who charged Our signs with falsehood; for they were a blind people."

Gen. 7:23 "Every living thing on the face of the earth was wiped out; men and animals and the creatures that move along the ground and the birds of the air were wiped from the face of the earth. Only Noah was left, and those with him in the ark."

Sura VIII:45–46 "Remember when God shewed them to thee in thy dream, as few: Had he shown them numerous, ye would certainly have become fainthearted, and would certainly have disputed the matter-But from this God kept you-He knoweth the very secrets of the breast.-And when, on your meeting, He made them appear to your eyes as few, and diminished you in their eyes, that God might carry out the thing that was to be done."

Dt. 20:8 "Then the officers shall add, "Is any man afraid or fainthearted? Let him go home so that his brothers will not become disheartened too."

He. 11:32 "And what more shall I say? I do not have time to tell about Gideon, Samson, Japethah, David, Samuel and the prophets, who through faith conquered kingdoms, administered justice, and gained what was promised; who shut the mouths of lions, quenched the fury of the flames, and escaped the edge of the sword; whose weakness was turned to strength; and routed foreign armies."

Sura IX:110 **"Which of the two is best? He who hath founded his building on the fear of God and the desire to please Him, or he who hath founded his building on the brink of an undermined bank washed away by torrents, so that it rusheth with him into the fire of Hell?"**

Mt. 7:26 "But everyone who hears these words of mine and does not put them into practice is like the foolish man who built his house on sand. The rain came down, the streams rose, and the winds blew and beat against that house, and it fell with a great crash."

Sura X:100 **"No soul can believeth but by the permission of God: and He shall lay his wrath on those who will not understand."**

Eph. 2:8, 9 "For it is by grace you have been saved, through faith — and this not from yourselves, it is the gift of God — not by works, so that no one can boast."

Rom. 2:5 "But because of your stubbornness and your unrepentant heart, you are storing up wrath against yourself for the day of God's wrath, when his righteous judgment will be revealed."

Sura XI:86 "O my people! Give weight and measure with fairness; purloin not other men's goods; and perpetrate not injustice on the earth with corrupt practices."

Deut. 25:13 "Do not have two differing weights in your bag—one heavy, one light. Do not have two differing measures in your house—one large, one small. You must have accurate and honest weights and measures."

Prov. 11:1 "The Lord abhors dishonest scales, but accurate weights are his delight."

Sura XIV:31 "And an evil word is like an evil tree torn up from the face of the earth, and without strength to stand."

Ps. 34:13 "Keep your tongue from evil and your lips from speaking lies."

Mt. 3:10 "The ax is already at the root of the trees, and every tree that does not produce good fruit will be cut down and thrown into the fire."

Surah XV:26 "We created man of dried clay, of dark loam moulded."

Gen.1:26 "And God said, let us make man in our image."

Gen. 4:19 "For out of it (dust) wast you taken: for dust thou art, and unto dust shalt thou return."

Sura XVI:44 **"They who bear ills with patience and put their trust in the Lord!"**

Rom. 5:3 "And not only so, but we glory in tribulations also: knowing that tribulation worketh patience."

Jam. 1:3 "Knowing this, that the trying of your faith worketh patience."

Sura XXIII:64 **"We will not burden a soul beyond its power: and with Us is a book which speaketh the truth; and they shall not be wronged."**

1 Cor. 10:13 "There hath no temptation taken you but such as is common to man: but God is faithful, who will not suffer you to be tempted above that ye are able; but will with the temptation also make a way to escape, that ye may be able to bear it."

Sura XXVII:55 **"And Lot, when he said to his people, "What! Proceed ye to such filthiness with your eyes open? What! Come ye with lust unto men rather than to women.**

Gen. 19: "And Lot went out at the door unto them, and shut the door after him, and said, I pray you brethren, do not so wickedly. Behold now, I have two daughters which have not known man; I pray you, bring them out unto you, and do ye to them as is good in your eyes: only do nothing; for therefore came they under the shadow of my roof."

Sura XXXV:42 "Yea, thou shalt not find any variableness in the way of God."

Mal. 3:6 "For I am the Lord, I change not; therefore ye sons of Jacob are not consumed."

Heb. 13:8 "Jesus Christ the same yesterday, and today, and for ever."

Sura XLII:39 "And there shall be no way *open* against those who, after being wronged, avenge themselves."

Rom. 12:19 "Dearly beloved, avenge not yourselves: for it is written ... Vengeance is mine; I will repay, saith the Lord."

Heb. 10:30 "For we know him that hath said, Vengeance belongeth to me, I will recompense, saith the Lord."

Sura XLIII:61 "And he (Jesus) shall be a sign of the *Last* Hour; doubt not then of it, and follow ye Me: this is the right way."

Jn. 14:18, 19 "I will not leave you comfortless: I will come to you. Yet a little while, and the world seeth me no more; but ye see me: because I live, ye shall live also."

Acrs 15:16 "After this I will return, and will build again the tabernacle of David, which is fallen down; and I will build again the ruins thereof, and I will set it up."

Sura LIII:34 "He well knew you when He produced you out of the earth, and when ye were embryos in your mother's womb."

Ps. 139:13 "For thou hast possessed my reins: thou hast covered me in my mother's womb."

Jer. 1:5 "Before I formed thee in the belly I knew thee; and before thou camest forth out of the womb I santified thee ..."

Sura LVII:19 "Know ye that this world's life is only a sport, and pastime, and show, and a cause of vainglory among you!"

Ecc. 3:1 "To every thing there is a season, and a time to every purpose under the heaven: a time to be born, and a time to die ..."

Ecc.12:7, 8 "Then shall the dust return to the earth as it was: and the spirit shall return unto God who gave it. Vanity of vanities, saith the preacher; all is vanity."

Sura LXII:1 "All that is in the heavens, and all that is on the earth, uttereth the praise of God, the King! The Holy!"

Ps. 145:10 "All thy works shall praise thee, O Lord; and thy saints shall bless thee."

Lk. 2:13 "And suddenly there was with the angel a multitude of the heavenly host praising God ..."

Sura LXV:7 "Let him who hath abundance give of his abundance; let him, too, whose store is scanty, give of what God hath vouchsafed to him. God imposes burdens only according to the means which He hath given."

Mrk. 12:43, 44 "That this poor widow hath cast more in, than they which have cast into the treasury; For all they did cast in of their abundance; but she of her want did cast in all that she had, even of her living."

2 Cor. 8:2 "How that in a great trial of affliction the abundance of their joy and their deep poverty abounded unto riches of their liberality."

Sura LXVIII:45 **"Yet will I bear long with them; for my plan is sure."**

1 Chr. 16:34 "O give thanks unto the Lord; for he is good: for his mercy endureth for ever."

1 Pet. 1:25 "But the word of the Lord endureth for ever. And this is the word which by the gospel is preached to you."

Sura LXXIII:14 **"The day cometh when the earth and the mountains shall be shaken; and the mountains shall become a loose sand heap."**

Ez. 38:19, 20 "Surely in that day there shall be a great shaking in the land of Israel; and the mountains shall be thrown down, and the steep places shall fall, and every wall shall fall to the ground."

Sura XCIV:1–3 **"Have We not OPENED thine heart for thee? And taken off from thee thy burden, which galled thy back?"**

Ps. 55:22 "Cast thy burden upon the Lord, and he shall sustain thee ..."

Mt. 11:28–30 "Come unto me, all ye that labour and are heavy ladden, and I will give you rest. Take my yoke upon you, and learn of me; for I am meek and lowly in heart: and ye shall find rest unto your souls. For my yoke is easy, and my burden is light."

Sura CVII:7, 8 **"Who make a show of devotion, but refuse help to the needy."**

Mt. 6:5 "And when thou prayest, thou shalt not be as the hypo-crites are: for they love to pray standing in the synagogues and in the corners of the streets, that they may be seen of men."

Job. 24:4 "They turn the needy out of the way: the poor of the earth hide themselves together."

NOTES

Chapter 1

1. Investigative Project on Terrorism, "Zaid Shakir:Cofounder, Zaytuna College," *Discoverthenetworks.org*, January 2011, http://discoverthenetworks.org/individualProfile.asp?indid=974.
2. Ryan Mauro, "Islamist U?," *FrontPageMag.com*, Wednesday, May 27, 2009: http://frontpagemag.com/readArticle.aspx?ARTID=35008.
3. Sahih al-Bukhari, "Abu Huraira, 6924, 6925, Book 88, Hadith 7," *Sunnah.com*, http://sunnah.com/bukhari/88.
4. Sunan Abi Dawud, "Ikrimah, 4351, Book 40, Hadith 1," *Sunnah.com*, http://sunnah.com/abudawud/40.
5. Sahih al-Bukari, "Ikrima, 6922, Book 88, Hadith 5, *Sunnah.com*, http://sunnah.com/bukhari/88.
6. James M. Arlandson, "Muhammad's atrocity against the Qurayza Jews," *Answering Islam*, http://www.answering-islam.org/Authors/Arlandson/qurayza_jews.htm.
7. James M. Arlandson ," Top Ten reasons why Islam is NOT the religion of peace," *Answering Islam*, http://www.answering-islam.org/Authors/Arlandson//ten_reasons.htm.

8. Michael Youseff, *Jesus, Jihad and Peace*, (Tennessee: Worthy Publishing, 2015), 111–113.
9. David Bukay, "Peace or Jihad? Abrogation in Islam," *Middle East Quarterly*, (Fall 2007): 3–11, http://www.meforum.org/1754/peace-or-jihad-abrogation-in-islam.
10. F. E. Peters, *Jesus & Muhammad*, (New York: Oxford University Press, first edition, 2010), 27.
11. John D. Clare, "The Crusades," accessed May 16, 2016, http://johndclare.net/KS3/1–3-6.htm.
12. Chris Armstrong, "Crusades and Inquisition: Part of a pattern of Christian violence?" *Grateful To The Dead: A church historian's playground*, last modified March 19, 2010, http://gratfultothedead.wordpress.com/2010/03/19/crusades-and-inquisition-part-of-a-pattern-of-christian-violence/.
13. Phyllis Chesler, "Leave and We'll Kill You: Islam and Apostates in America," *Pajamas Media*, last modified August 2, 2010, http://www.phyllis-chesler.com/832/islam-apostates-in-america.
14. Phyllis Chesler "Are Honor Killings Simply Domestic Violence?" *Middle East Quarterly* 16, no. 2(Spring 2009): 61–69. http://www.meforum.org/2067/are-honor-killings-simply-domestic-violence.
15. "Remember America's Lost Women: Create a National Day of Memory for Women and Girls Killed in the Name of Honor," *Change.org*, accessed May 16, 2016, https://www.Change.org/p/remember-america-s-lost-women-create-a-national-day-of-memory-for-women-and-girls-killed-in-the-name-of-honor.
16. Chesler, "Are Honor Killings Violence?" 3.
17. Phyllis Chesler, "Worldwide Trends in Honor Killings," *Middle East Quarterly*, 17, no 2 (Spring 2010): 3, http://www.meforum.org/2646/worldwide-trends-honor-killings.
18. David P. Goldman, "Jihad and Self-Sacrifice in Islam," *PJ Media*, February 16, 2015,

http://pjmedia.com/spengler/2015/02/16/
jihad-and-self-sacrifice-in-islam/?print=1.

19. Abul Kasem, , "Incest in Islam," *The Real Islam,* December
1, 2010, http://www.real-islam.com/abulkasem/incest-in-
islam.htm.

20. Dimitrius and Sam Shamoun, "Islam and Adultery: An
Examination of Muhammad's Marriage Privileges,"
Answering Islam, accessed May 18, 2016, http://www.
answering-islam.org/Shamoun/privileges.htm.

21. Ami Isseroff, "Sayyid Qutb," Encyclopedia of the Middle
East, December 7, 2008, http://www.mideastweb.org/Middle-
East-Encyclopedia/sayyid_qutb.htm

Chapter 3

1. Roger Barrier, "Were There Any Women Bible
Writers?" *Ask Roger,* last accessed, May 18,
2016, http://preachitteachtit.org/ask-roger/detail/
were-there-any-women-bible-writers/.

2. Jeffrey Kranz and Laura Kranz, "The 35 authors who
wrote the Bible," *Overview Bible,* accessed May 18, 2016,
http://overviewbible.com/authors-who-wrote-bible/.

3. "Preservation of the Quran (part 2 of 2): The Written
Koran," *The Religion of Islam,* last modified December
4, 2014, http://islamreligion/articles/18/.

4. Samuel Green, "Comparing The Bible And The Qur'an:
How to do it accurately,"*Answering Islam,* last modified
March 8, 2016, http://www.answering-islam.org/Green/
compare.htm.

5. Bernard Ramm, *Protestant Christian Evidences,*
(Chicago,:Moody Press, 1953),11.

6. Nabeel Quershi, Seeking *Allah, Finding Jesus,* (Grand
Rapids: Zondervan, 2014), 230.

7. Ibid, 234.

8. John Gilchrist, "Is Muhammad Foretold in the Bible?" *Answering Islam,* accessed May 18, 2016, http://www.answering-islam.org/Gilchrist/muhammad.html.
9. Querishi, *Seeking Alla,* 240.
10. Dr. W. Campbell, "The Bible As Seen By The Qur'an And The Muslim Traditions," *Answering Islam,* accessed May 18, 2016, http://www.answering-islam.org/Campbell/s2c1.html.
11. Joe Musser, James C. Hefley, and Marti Hefley, *Fire On The Hills: the Rochunga Paudite story,* (Illinois: Tyndale House Publishers, 1999), 230.

Chapter 4

1. John Piper, *Finally Alive,* (Scotland, Great Britian: Christian Focus Publications, 2009), 12.
2. Brooks Egerton, "Fort Hood captain: Hasan wanted patients to face war crimes charges," *Dallas Morning News,* last modified November 26, 2010, http://www.dallasnews.com/news/20091117-fort-Hood-captain-Hasan-wanted-9439.ece.
3. CBS News, "New details emerge on Canada shooting suspect," *CBS This Morning,* last modified October 23, 2014, http://www.cbsnews.com/news/ottawa-shooting-investigation-continues-unclear-if-gunman-had-accomplices/.
4. Ryan Parry, "Muslim convert 'who beheaded colleague' is charged with murder as it emerges he returned to Oklahoma food plant for 'revenge' after he was fired earlier that day for 'not liking white people,'" *Daily Mail,* last modified October, 1, 2014, http://www.dailymail.co.uk/news/article-2775194/Oklahoma-man-charged-murder-beheading.html.
5. Joe Musser, James C. Hefley, and Marti Hefley, *Fire On The Hills: the Rochunga Paudite story,* (Illinois: Tyndale House Publishers, Inc, 1999), 243.

6. Michael Youseff, *Jesus, Jihad and Peace*, (Tennessee: Worthy Publishing, 2015), 173.

7. Mosab Hassan Yousef, "Son of Hammas: (Illinois: Tyndale House Publishers, Inc, 2011), 83.

Chapter 5

1. C.S. Lewis, "Studies In Words," (Cambridge, United Kingdom: Cambridge University Press, 2013), 7.

Chapter 6

1. Chris Nichols, "Living the Conversion Continuum," pp.3, http://www.nicholspage.org/blog1/?_id=55

Epilogue

1. David Limbauge, "Jesus On Trial," (Washington, D.C.: Regnery Publishing, 2014), 339.

CPSIA information can be obtained
at www.ICGtesting.com
Printed in the USA
FSOW01n0555180716
22806FS